RUN FRO

Final Update: Book 1

ALLEN KUZARA

"Device assisted meditation marks the dawn of a new era in human development which will allow for heretofore unseen levels of achievement, productivity, and personal happiness."

Josh Zander—CEO of DataMind

"Better is the end of a thing than the beginning thereof..."

Ecclesiastes 7:8 KJV

FAIRBANKS

CHAPTER 1

NICK STOOD IN front of his parent's dining room table in the dark. He peered through the tightly drawn curtains in numb stupefaction, watching his across-the-street neighbor, Mrs. Lambert, make her final lapse in judgement.

Maybe it was senility, or maybe it was desperation and the need for the world to go back to something normal. Whether Mrs. Lambert knew what she was doing or not, it was suicide. And Nick was watching it happen in slow-motion.

Mrs. Lambert had her kitchen light on, the auxiliary light over her sink of dirty dishes that she was attempting to wash. She couldn't have picked a worse light to turn on in the house. It was a beacon to the outside world. A lighthouse, except no lives were being saved today.

She wouldn't even finish the dishes, Nick knew. And there was nothing he could do about it either.

Well, he could try to stop them. He might even have initial success with the single-shot shotgun he carried slung over his back. But soon enough, the sound of the gunshots would attract more crazies than he could fight off and they would get him and, maybe, Mrs. Lambert to boot. Firing on them was just as much a suicidal act as what Mrs. Lambert was doing.

He thought about looking the other way, going on down into the basement with the supplies he'd grabbed and trying to forget what was about to happen. But he couldn't bring himself to turn away from the head-on collision, the slow-motion train wreck he was certain was about to happen.

It began. Like alley cats creeping out of the shadows, former residents and strangers alike moved toward Mrs. Lambert's home. They seemed aware of each other but maintained their shared focus: Mrs. Lambert. Of all the things to cooperate on, Nick thought.

Nick didn't dare open his window, but he could faintly hear Mrs. Lambert humming a tune over the sound of water running in the sink. Then as one of the crazies approached from the road, a more direct and visible ingress, Mrs. Lambert dropped her scrub brush and let out a squeal of panic.

Nick watched as she futilely turned off her light and water. It was too late. The beasts were at her door now, pounding and kicking. The one from the road ran, jumped, and found purchase on her still opened window. Nick saw one of the long-haired females punch in a window on the side of Mrs. Lambert's house and begin to climb through the remaining shards. The rest of the crazies seemed to notice the successful entry point and ran to the window.

Then Nick heard Mrs. Lambert's final scream. He knew it was almost over, at least for her. They were killing her in the most brutal way, bludgeoning her to death with their fists and feet. And that was if she was lucky. Nick had seen someone torn limb from limb, like a sick game of tug-of-war, the first day after the update.

Nick had seen enough. Too much. He wanted to go on down to the basement. He almost rationalized his wish, thinking he could go now while there was a good distraction. The old coal pit had been turned into a basement in the sixties when everyone in Fairbanks, Alaska had changed to propane or natural gas. Its entrance was outside, down steps between the house's front door and the door to the detached garage.

He could probably make it, he told himself. Nick, however, was too level-headed, too much of a planner to respond to his base impulse. He knew what would happen next, what the crazies would do when they were finished with Mrs. Lambert. They would turn on each other. Then they would kill until there was only one left, one almost human champion. Nick knew it wouldn't be over until he saw a single crazy walk out of the house. He would have to wait until the champion left and was out of sight before descending the outdoor stairs to the basement.

Survival after the world went broke was a numbers game, he had decided. It was all about ratios. The fewer of them nearby, the better his chances were. And time was on his side. As far as he could tell, the crazies were barely animals, let alone humans. They acted on singular instincts, namely rage and aggression, but weren't balanced out like natural creatures with impulses to gather food, hibernate, migrate, reproduce, etc. If Nick and anyone else not affected by the update could just hang on long enough, the crazies would all either starve, kill each other off, or die in this year's coming winter.

Nick watched Mrs. Lambert's motionless, soundless house. He knew what was happening inside, but on the exterior, everything looked normal, happy even. And that was exactly like people were before the update. The app they'd used had made them happier, more productive people. But deep down somewhere inside lay dormant all the suppressed hate that was now so visible in the world.

Nick waited patiently and watched what he'd predicted come true. The last wild-eyed man exited Mrs. Lambert's house. He didn't look back and he didn't close the door as he walked out. He seemed to have no awareness or conscious reflection about what he had just done. Instead he casually strolled down the street toward the next brawl.

Nick thought he heard a window crash somewhere. Apparently, the wild man did too, because he picked up his pace like a hound picking up a fresh scent.

Nick had seen this all before, more times in the last three days than he cared to admit. And it was happening over and over, simultaneously, in hundreds, maybe thousands of places all over the globe.

CHAPTER 2

NICK AND JIMMY spent most of their time down in the basement. This wasn't really anything new to them. Many of their adolescent years had been spent down in this damp, dingy dungeon. Especially Nick's. Jimmy was Nick's stepbrother, younger by one and a half years.

Nick's mom was out there somewhere. She left his dad one day out of the blue when Nick was nine. Since then, it had been an occasional unannounced drop-in visit, birthday and Christmas cards—most years—and not much else. Nick's dad and Jimmy's mom met and were married a few years after when Nick and Jimmy were twelve and ten. Those were the early years of Nick's family's most recent iteration, only a handful of years after Nick's Grandpa Joe had died and left his dad the house and most of its contents— almost all of which remained untouched, unchanged in the basement and garage. Nick had decided his dad had left it that way as some kind of shrine to the old man.

Even Jimmy who had never met Grandpa Joe had a fondness for his memory. Before the world "went broke"—the commonly used term for the hellish phenomenon of the last three days—Grandpa Joe's "lair," as the boys had called it, had been a mysterious place full of tools and memorabilia; each newly discovered item seemed to demand that the boys spend at least half a day (a pre-pubescent eternity) imagining what, when, where, and why. It had been beyond ideal.

Now, after the world went broke, Grandpa Joe's basement had become, yet again, the boys' sanctuary. This time it wasn't a place for the boys to dream, it was a place for them to escape the nightmare of the real world that continued to unfold on their doorstep. This time it was for very real, practical reasons: the basement had only one way in and one way out, there was little that could catch on fire, and— perhaps most importantly—Grandpa Joe's HAM radio gear was down there, still hooked up, still cranking out fifteen-hundred watts when they squeezed the handle of the transceiver microphone unit.

Just like years ago when Nick and Jimmy had first discovered the radio unit, they were mostly just listening, scanning the frequency bands and picking up bits and pieces of news from all around the world. Back then it had been because it was technically illegal to broadcast without a HAM operator's license. The two had never heard of anyone getting in serious trouble over it, but the you'll-go-to-jail warning from Nick's dad was enough to keep the pirate transmissions down to a once-a-week infraction. It was like the prank calls before caller-ID and cell phones. As long as you didn't do it too much, too often, you were fine.

Nick remembered the first time they had picked up a transmission coming out of Tokyo. At least, the boys had decided it was from Tokyo; all they knew back then was that it wasn't English, Spanish, or Russian— the only three languages they had, until then, heard on shortwave. The radio, with Grandpa Joe's embarrassingly large antenna on a tall tower in the back, had been a seemingly forbidden connection to the rest of the world.

The boys couldn't remember a time before the internet. And they could barely remember life before their parents had smart phones. You would think the radio would have lost its magic on such hi-tech, well connected youths, but the opposite was true. The analog, static-ridden electronics, the lack of repeatable or predictable experiences, the fact that everything was live, happening right then but not right there—they had been mesmerized.

Now, the radio was no longer a magical, enchanted relic; it was their chance to stay alive, to keep and stay ahead of what might be coming next. It was their all too real lifeline.

They didn't have the HAM history firmly in mind and hadn't really been told much about it, except that it had predated the web and was practiced by a dying breed of old codgers who'd seen better days. By the time they were old enough to look it up online, the radio and much of Grandpa Joe's lair was already a buried memory, some childish fancy that might be remembered briefly from time to time, even talked about with fondness, but not a viable place to go and make new memories.

Nick stood briefly in the breezeway between the house and the garage where the basement stairs were. There was a draft there. Always had been for as long as he could remember. He felt like staying there and cooling down in the mild but hot Alaskan July. But this was a dangerous place to be: outside, exposed to the street. He had waited until the rampaging crazy that had attacked Mrs. Lambert was gone and he couldn't see or hear anyone else. But he couldn't stand there long. Not unless he wanted to end up like Mrs. Lambert.

They were *not* zombies, he told himself. Why that made him feel any better, he didn't know. They weren't undead, and they couldn't take deadly blows and keep on coming. They were just angry humans . . . sort of.

He proceeded quietly down the steps, listening for signs of danger as he went. Summer in Fairbanks was a lovely time of year. At least he wasn't crunching through snow and ice, but he did have to deal with the eternal sun. Even now at a 11:45 PM, the sun glowed near the horizon. It would have been nice to have the cover of darkness, but Nick would leave the wishing to someone else. Jimmy did enough wishing for both of them.

Nick's hair stood up on the back of his neck as he stepped down to the landing at the bottom of the stairs. His animal instincts told him there was danger: he heard sounds. But quickly he realized it was just Jimmy and the radio inside. "He's going to get us killed," he whispered. As softly but as quickly as he could, Nick opened the windowless door with his key. The door was thick, heavy, the kind of doors they don't make any more, back from the day when old-growth heartwood was still an affordable commodity. They had wisely taken both of the key rings their parents had kept stashed away in a kitchen drawer and had each put one on a long string to wear around their necks.

Nick went in and locked the door behind him. Then he dropped the homemade locking bar—a two-by-four—across the door and secured it to the bracing on each side. They had attached the bracing by hand with a screwdriver (they couldn't risk pounding nails or using an electric drill.) Nick rushed over to Jimmy and the radio and turned the volume down so low it was almost inaudible. Jimmy twisted it back halfway to where it had been and gave Nick a dirty look.

Voices whispered over the radio. When it all started to come apart, the boys had turned on TV and watched the mayhem. The networks hadn't stayed on long. When Alan Tanner, the local Channel Six newscaster and local celebrity, went broke on live television—well, that had been the sign to all the other local affiliates to give it up. The boys had switched to local radio which only lasted a couple of hours longer. When those went black, they had switched to shortwave and found the BBC still reporting. But now that the "B" was out, all that was left were individual HAMs, people in as big a jam as they were, many of whom were also stowed away in some cellar, attic, or bunker waiting out the end of the world.

Nick recognized some of the voices. Jimmy had been hanging out near this frequency band since yesterday. These voices, Nick could tell, weren't the scared witless amateurs they had heard before who had somehow figured out how to transmit an SOS-Mayday-Someone-oh-someone-please-come-save-me message. These guys were older HAMs who seemed totally comfortable with the situation, almost like they'd expected it to happen eventually, and were just slightly bummed-out that they had to deal with it.

Nick knew a couple of the voices. There was a guy from South Florida who liked to talk about getting on his sailboat if things got any worse. There was a woman in Alberta—she was the only female crashing this boys' club, but no one seemed to mind. And then there was a gruff sounding fellow from Denver who commented infrequently, but when he did, they were bombshells of negativity. Not panic, mind you. Just big ol' piles of reality that left their stench on the conversation for ten minutes at a time—a veritable eternity for an active shortwave channel.

"Anything new?" Nick asked Jimmy.

"It's getting worse," Jimmy answered. Nick listened in on the HAMs' conversation.

[If you ask me, they had it coming to them. This generation has been the most spoiled, most entitled bunch of brats the world has ever seen. The sorry thing is that we're, yet again, the ones who will have to clean up the mess.] *Alberta

[You forgot to mention lazy.] *Denver

[You guys are right. No question there. But I'm still confused—call it a senior moment—how this could affect so many people. It wasn't just twenty-five-year-olds, you know. Heck, I know people our age that went broke.] *South Florida

[Serves them right. They should have acted their age.] *Denver

16

[DataMind must have done this on purpose, or maybe it got hacked.] *South Florida

[Don't see why anyone would wish this on their worst enemy. No, it was an unintended consequence, hubris at its worst. And mother nature has had the last word.] *Alberta

. . .

The conversation went on endlessly like this: old farts chatting the night away. DataMind was the name of the smartphone app that had brought down the world. But it didn't start out that way, not by a long shot. Its first version had gone viral among the self-help/motivational blogosphere, and by the time version 2.0 was released, the business world had embraced the app with open arms and clenched fists. Why clenched fists? Because they saw green. Major Benjamins.

DataMind had been marketed as an app that aided in the practice of secular meditation. But this was an understatement. And just like a good car salesman, the creators of DataMind had let the world look under the hood, see for themselves what the app could really do before they asked anyone to sign on the dotted line. The developers had offered the app for free for thirty days after which you could subscribe for updates at $2.99 a month. It didn't take long for the rave reviews of each month's new update, how the developers had outdone themselves again and again, for people to get

17

it: the updates were the best three bucks you would spend in your whole life.

When a few holdouts (people too cheap to subscribe to the updates) complained that the app didn't seem to work as well as it did when they first bought it, the rest of the world was intolerant. They lashed out at them on social media for how, if they were too cheap to pay three bucks to be a better person, then they were scum and didn't deserve to use the app anyway. No one seemed to pay attention to the symptoms described by these hold-out users: headaches, insomnia, and other conditions. The holdouts were regarded as little more than internet trolls. It was a brave new world, and there was no time to be bothered with insignificant insubstantialities or losers.

The real reason for the app's success and the reason everyone working a job had made DataMind synonymous with a life worth living had been that these *meditation* sessions, as they were called, did much more than refresh one's mind. Of course, researchers had known for years that increased mindfulness achieved through various forms of meditation could translate into higher productivity and a general sense of well-being on the part of the meditator. But DataMind's sessions had moved people from amateur status to Dalai Lama level meditators in just a couple of sessions with benefits so extreme, so exciting that the app became indispensable.

The studies demonstrating the positive effect of the app fell far behind everyday practice, because each month (later they were released bi-weekly) the updates for the app increased the benefits over the previous version. It was as if each update was a seine through which yet more mental gunk and grime was squeezed out of the user's mind, leaving them increasingly refreshed and more capable in almost every way.

The research, despite its lagging nature, proved that IQs were almost instantaneously increased by a margin of 10% above base level. And each session only heightened the individual's cognitive abilities.

A smarter world would have been enough of an achievement to turn the app developers into instant billionaires, but a boost of intelligence was only a small piece of the package. The euphoria experienced after just the first session was on the level of an illicit drug. That's the *real* reason DataMind's reputation had spread as fast as it did. It would have been wildly successful had it just been extremely fun. All the dumb, addicting adult game apps had proven that. But the euphoria, often described as true peace, the first peace many users claimed to have ever experienced in their lives, was what pushed the app into the sales stratosphere. The powerful testimonials were compelling especially because they were coming from people like your boss or your next-door neighbor instead of some washed-up former celebrity on a three o'clock in the morning infomercial.

So, peace and intelligence are a pretty popping duo, but what about needing less sleep? Like, three hours a night? Or weight loss? People being able to finally, after decades of failing to do so, stick to a healthy diet and drop thirty pounds in six months. And not complain or be miserable in the process.

Even the third world was catching on, seeing the app as their only way out of poverty. The crazy thing was that it actually seemed to work, a fact that represented a real sore spot for certain political pundits who saw these masses as being helpless, hopeless victims without any internal resources. Yes, the world was becoming a bright, squeaky-clean version of itself with no end in sight for the perceived advances being experienced by literally billions.

Fortunately for Nick and Jimmy, the app had an adult-only warning; it actually made you prove your age through the use of a credit card in your name instead of just making you click some box swearing you were eighteen or older. But this wasn't because DataMind didn't want to get kids hooked; they had plans to increase their market share to include the two demographics that were least likely to use the app: kids and senior adults. The seniors didn't adopt DataMind for the same reason they don't adopt lots of things: old people are set in their ways and proud of it. The kids, however, were prohibited due to the unknown impact on their development. All the creators needed early on was some string of teen suicides, an easy to find happenstance, to shut them down in a hurry.

Then the world went broke on that fateful Friday afternoon. The biweekly updates had come out on Fridays at eight a.m. eastern time, which meant it was only four in the morning in Alaska. But that didn't matter. Like junkies jonesing for their next fix, people set their alarms all around the world so they could enjoy the benefits of the latest release. For these people, the updated version of the app was worth getting up in the middle of the night. It wasn't like they needed eight uninterrupted hours of sleep anyway.

Whatever it was, a bug, a glitch, bio-digital terrorism—the impact was felt instantaneously; the first symptom, the first complaint—and really their last— was that this update wasn't as good as the previous one. In fact, it didn't really work at all. Most people said they had headaches, that they'd even lost some of their abilities. News headlines flashed all over the internet and television: DATAMIND MISSED THE MARK and UPDATE FAIL.

How little did they know how right they were. People scrambled to reload the old version of the app to see if it would undo the losses, to at least help people get back where they had been. The number one search engine term that day (also a news headline) was RELOAD OLD VERSION DATAMIND.

Who knows? Maybe some people were actually successful, but if they were, it was too little too late. Within a couple hours after the update, there were reports of violent psychotic breaks occurring. It probably happened even sooner than that, but it took a couple hours before the staunch believers could accept the fact that the update had caused the breaks. One by one, pieces of the social machinery, people from every industry, class, and sector, *went broke*. That was the term that in short order was used to describe the whole fiasco.

Nick and Jimmy had been home when it all went down, glued to the news feed on TV and online. It was exciting in a weird way; the way older kids and even adults enjoy the oncoming blizzard or hurricane. Danger breathed some new life into them, albeit temporarily. They had tried to reach their parents. When their calls went through—usually the system was so overloaded they didn't—they went straight to voicemail. They tried to rationalize this, saying that the phones weren't really ringing, that the cell towers probably weren't even working properly and that the system just sent their calls to voicemail. But deep down, they knew the truth. At least Nick did; their parents had gone broke like all the other users of the app.

That was three long days ago. The world had changed so much, so permanently in that period of time that Nick, although he tried, had trouble clearly remembering life before the update.

Nick slowly surfaced from his interior self, first hearing the higher pitches of the radio, then hearing the still unintelligible gestalt and sound, and like eyes refocusing on a near object, he listened to the words spoken.

"Who on there is closest to us?" Nick asked Jimmy who seemed to have been enthralled by the radio, with rapt attention.

"Some guy named Bob," Jimmy answered.

"Where?" Nick mouthed as if the HAMs could hear them talking.

"Up in Deadhorse. Pretty close." Jimmy half-grinned.

"I guess. I mean, that's closer than Florida, but I'd hate to try to walk there."

"Hey, we should try to talk to him."

"Who?" Nick asked perplexed.

"Bob. He's not that far. Maybe he knows where we should go, or—who knows? He's the closest sane person we know. Except for Mrs. Lambert, but a lot of help she would be."

Nick tried to hide his grimace at the mention of Mrs. Lambert. He hadn't told Jimmy, and he didn't plan on doing so.

"What if some crazy is listening and figures out where we are?" Nick asked.

"Really? You think they are sitting at home listening to shortwave?"

"There could be unaffected people listening. People like us that are desperate enough to…"

"The most dangerous thing right now is isolation," Jimmy said with self-evidential confidence.

"Hardly," Nick replied. But he let it go.

Jimmy waited for a pause in the radio chatter, then he squeezed his pale fingers around the transceiver microphone. "This is Jimmy Donovan in Fairbanks, Alaska. Anyone got your ears on?"

Nick winced when Jimmy gave away their city locale and then again when he used the dumb CB-trucker jargon.

There was silence. Then the voice from Denver said, "What's your callsign?"

Jimmy twisted his head over to Nick. Of course, Nick thought. You start this and turn to me when you don't know what to do. Nick tried to think. There was something there, some clue deep down in the recesses of his childhood memories. Then he had it.

He pointed at the wall where Grandpa Joe's plaque hung. "Try that," he said.

"You want me to read Grandpa Joe's plaque to them?"

24

"No," Nick said jumping up and moving to the wall. He read the award: This here certifies that Joseph Thatcher (#AD3CRD) has attained the notable achievement of relaying multiple stations on...

"AD3CRD. Try that," Nick said.

Jimmy spoke the callsign cautiously.

More static.

"Well, that's not *your* callsign, but I am interested to know where you got that. This is Bob in Deadhorse, since we don't all seem to be licensed HAMs for the moment. I guess the FCC has enough trouble on their hands right now. Don't suppose they'll come after us anytime soon."

Nick thought he heard the geezer chuckle at his own comment before releasing the microphone switch.

"My brother and I are using my Grandpa Joe's radio," Jimmy confessed.

"You're Joe's grandkids?" Bob said. "Well, I'll be. Never thought I'd be hearing someone over Joe's unit again. Say, how are you two fairing in Fairbanks?"

"About like everyone else in the big cities. As long as we keep quiet with the lights off, we're okay."

"When are you planning to get out of there?"

Jimmy looked at Nick. This was something they'd quarreled over already and with no clear winner.

"We're still working on that," Jimmy answered. "My brother Nick doesn't think it's safe yet."

"I'd say he's right. The problem is, it's only going to get more dangerous if things go the way I expect them to," Bob said. "You know, we're the lucky ones here in Alaska. The closest nuclear reactor is in Russia, over a thousand miles west. And if I know those Ruskies—and I do—they didn't all buy into the hype around DataMind. Shoot, I know there was probably a Russian translated app, but I bet not one in a hundred downloaded it over there. You know, they don't really like being happy. It's too unrealistic. If somebody is all smiles, they look at them like they're crazy, weak-minded or something. Who knows? Maybe they're right after all. Most people figure it's just the cold that makes them that way, but it's plenty cold in Alaska, and you boys know firsthand how many people swallowed that DataMind crap hook, line, and sinker."

"Ask him what he meant about the reactors," Nick said sotto-voce. Ordinarily this rambling type would annoy Nick, but except for the fact that he felt it was critical Bob finished his thought about the nukes, Nick enjoyed hearing him go on. As doom-and-gloom as the situation was, Bob seemed impervious.

"What about the reactors?" Jimmy asked.

"Oh, yeah. Well, I hate to talk about it in front of the fellows who will have to face this head on, but they already know what they're in for. Some parts of the Gulf won't get hit too bad at first. But at some point, utilities will fail due to lack of workers. Mackey in Colorado—God bless his soul—is already transmitting off generators. But when the lights go out, best I can figure is you got three days in most places before the automatic emergency electrical generators used to cool the fuel rods of your neighborhood Mc-Nuke reactor run out of diesel and the reactor begins to melt down. Then you've got a hundred simultaneous Fukushimas on the North American continent."

Nick grabbed the microphone, "But you said we're not near a reactor. This is Nick by the way."

"Nick, you sound more like your Grandpa Joe than your brother does."

Nick didn't look at Jimmy, but he knew this would bother him. Nick was a blood-relative; Jimmy wasn't.

"That's true about the reactors," Bob continued. "But you're going to see some toxic brew swarming to the south of you. Most weather patterns move from west to east. But you've lived here long enough to know a storm can come in from any direction. I'm just suggesting you both get as far away from Dodge as you possibly can. Besides, even if the power stays on indefinitely, you can't possibly have more than a few weeks of food left in your house. Then what are you going to do?"

Bob was right, they'd already eaten all the crackers and chips in the house and were now relegated to the last dozen cans of Campbell's soup and a couple cans of tuna.

"Look," Bob continued, "I wouldn't bring all this up just to alarm you. Ignorance is bliss, and if I didn't have an idea on how to help Joe's grandkids I wouldn't have even mentioned all this. Morbid, I guess, but I figure it's better not to see some things coming if you can't do anything about it."

Now that the stakes had changed in Nick's mind, he was feeling less patient with Bob's ramblings.

"What should we do?" Nick asked.

There was a brief pause, and for a moment Nick wondered if they'd lost Bob's signal.

"Come to Deadhorse," Bob said finally. "I'm up here at the end of the Dalton Highway. If you follow it north until you run out of pavement, you'll see the pipeline continue on a pace. It heads toward a mountain, Mount Hubley, and then veers sharply east. If you follow the pipeline and keep heading toward the mountain, you'll run smack dab into the St. Victoria research station. We're at the foot of the mountain, and even during a snowstorm you ought to be able to see our beacon flashing. You're welcome up here boys. And you'll be safe."

Nick looked at Jimmy who seemed to be eating this with a spoon. He liked anything that would pull you out of your circumstances, any quick fix. Any fancy fantasy would do. Nick, on the other hand, saw nothing but reasons why this would fail: the distance to Deadhorse, the road conditions, a vehicle, fuel, getting lost, and were they really better off in Deadhorse with Bob?

"That's really nice of you," Jimmy said. "We'd be glad to…"

Nick grabbed the microphone out of Jimmy's hand who gave an injured look in return. "But we'll think about it. Give us a night to sleep on it," Nick finished.

Nick had no intention of going to Deadhorse, but he'd been around Jimmy long enough to pick up his cues. He knew if he didn't twist the screw slowly that the wood would split. Jimmy would do another one of his spas-out trips, and you never knew exactly what you'd be in for, just that you'd be in for a long, unpleasant headache if the storm, called Jimmy's episodes, was summoned forth. Jimmy usually seemed passive and withdrawn, but when he latched onto something, an idea that his bleeding heart believed in, he could throw the most massive tantrums.

"Boys, I've got everything you don't: isolation, tons of food, and barrels of diesel to keep the lights on for years. They send people up here and stock the station to the hilt. You're welcome any time, but realize the Dalton Highway's not going to be passable for too much longer. Once we start getting snow this fall, you'd need some heavy equipment to get up here. I don't suspect the truckers will be keeping it clear for us this year."

"Bob, we'll talk in the morning," Nick said, feigning a yawn. It didn't matter that it was after midnight. Nick and Jimmy had been on summer break and out of school long enough to have reverted to the teenage graveyard shift.

"Please do," Bob said. "I'll be counting on it. If I can help Joe's grandkids—well, that would be some silver lining to this whole mess we're in. Goodnight, boys."

CHAPTER 3

THE REST OF that night was spent chatting about Bob and Deadhorse before the two powered down and plugged into their cell phones. Nick permitted Jimmy to go on about it, knowing it was something he would have to get out of his system. More so that night than the next day when the excitement of the idea had worn off a bit.

Bedtime for the boys was no longer an arbitrary moment when the hour and minute hands lined up on their parents' clocks. Nick thought it strange though that what was obviously more natural, going to bed when you felt tired, meant that they ended up falling asleep later and later each night. And that was with all the TV channels down. Still, the internet was partially functioning. Most of the systems were programmed and therefor automatic, Nick figured. It was odd being able to stream top-dollar videos and movies with casts of actors that had surely gone broke and were probably dead already.

Too, Nick wondered how many other unaffected people in the world were watching the same shows they were. There was a certain sense of belonging, togetherness even—although he would never use those words out loud—about watching a show or movie that your friends at school were sure to watch and talk about the next day. Or even those huge multi-million viewer shows that made news headlines. You knew you weren't alone when you watched the most recent episode.

Now, and maybe forever, that was gone. Whatever was still up on the web—even things Nick had wanted to see before the update—was just another relic of the old world that would probably never come back around again.

Nick, headphones in and phone glowing brightly in his face, glanced up at Jimmy who was in the same kind of spot, curled up in what had become his part of the room: sleeping bag, pillow, some books, and his shoes pulled off on the floor next to him. Jimmy was plugged into his phone and the web too, partly because this is what teenagers did at all hours of the night, but also because this synthetic separation was the only real privacy the boys got from each other now.

Nick could remember when their parents had first met and how great he and Jimmy had gotten along.

After that first summer, Nick had been disappointed to find out Jimmy wouldn't be in any of his classes when school started back. But that phase hadn't lasted long. The differences between the boys emerged as they got older. And by the time Nick reached high school, neither of them were that excited by the other's company.

It was a regrettable situation, Nick believed. He wished he liked his brother more, but what could he do? And the feeling was mutual. Jimmy seemed totally disinterested in the things that got Nick going: cars, baseball, cool friends, and girls. Especially girls. It wasn't that Nick was a dumb jock—he got better grades than Jimmy usually did, after all. He was just good at more than one thing. There's no rule that says you only have to use your brain, or you only use your body. Nick wasn't a bookworm, but he did what he had to do to get the grades he was aiming for. That was it; he always knew what he wanted, and he laid the plans, the steps necessary to reach those goals.

Jimmy couldn't be more different. Jimmy was aimless, listless, indecisive. Except for things that seemed trivial to everyone else. He would latch onto these quirky, obtuse ideas and hang on for dear life. Their parents had thought it was just another phase, something Jimmy would grow out of eventually. Nick wasn't so sure. Jimmy found things that were, in his words, *fresh*. He'd get really into Kurusawa films, or the band Rush, or a new game marketed as a multi-player expandable universe. He'd do these things with all his might, all his focus and enthusiasm for a few weeks, becoming the world's imminent expert. And then, just as randomly as he fell into the mania, he'd fall out of it. Never to touch his obsession again.

Then the hunt would begin. That was the part that was so insufferable, much worse than the manic obsession once a new interest was found. The hunt, Nick's word for it, was that period when Jimmy was no longer infatuated with his old obsession—in fact, he was completely disillusioned by it. If you left him alone, then months or years later he could recount fondness for the subject. But if you pushed him about it right after he'd fallen out of love with the obsession, he would spew all kinds of bitter, sarcastic, spinster angst and never be able to think kindly of the subject ever again.

Nick had silently predicted that one day Jimmy's obsessive impulses would finally focus on a member of the opposite sex, but that day had never come. And Jimmy was sixteen, for crying out loud. Definitely old enough to have the heart-thumping, palm-sweating, stomach-sinking love intoxicating impulse that every young man experiences.

Nick wondered—no, feared is the right word— that Jimmy might be gay. Outwardly, Nick felt like he was supposed to think it was okay. To each, his own.

Live and let live, and all that stuff. But inwardly, he hated the idea. It wasn't because they were related; they didn't share any of the same blood, just stepparents. The idea, Nick knew, would mean Jimmy would be further tormented by kids at school, more than he was already. And besides, it was gross. Nick couldn't stand to think the thought, couldn't visualize the reality.

Nick watched Jimmy's eyes grow heavy as he drifted away to sleep, his phone still dancing light and images into the otherwise dark corner of the room. Jimmy seemed okay. . . for now, at least. This nightmare of events would be hard for anyone; it was certainly hard for Nick. And Jimmy, being the way he was, would struggle with it more than most. But the real reason Nick was concerned about his little brother was that he was a prescription drug user. No, not an abuser of prescription drugs—although Nick was pretty sure Jimmy smoked pot sometimes. His doctor gave Jimmy anti-depressants, and wouldn't you know it— Jimmy's mom was supposed to refill his prescription the day of the update. That meant this was the end of day three since Jimmy ran out of medication.

Nick didn't know what to expect, really. When he first realized the situation, he figured it meant Jimmy would get more sullen than normal, but then he read the back of the bottle and did an internet search on it. Anti-depressants weren't supposed to be stopped cold turkey. You were supposed to get weaned-off gradually. One of the possible side-effects of a sudden stop in medication was psychotic breaks and an increased risk of suicide. As if Nick didn't have enough on his plate. As if just staying alive wasn't hard enough. Now he felt like he was a prison warden on suicide watch.

CHAPTER 4

"NICK, WAKE UP!"

Nick felt the accompanying tug on his shirt, his sleeping bag having already been partially unzipped. He carefully opened his eyes, bracing himself for a room full of light. But what he saw was Jimmy standing over him with a pen light clipped to his t-shirt collar, light spraying Jimmy in the face like some weird psychedelic music video.

"What is it? What time is it?" Nick asked.

"The lights are off, Nick."

The tugging continued as if Nick wasn't really awake. "I can see that. What are you doing? Let go of my shirt."

"No, you don't get it," Jimmy said. "The power's off. The lights won't come on."

Nick reached for his phone. It was sad how he was still utterly dependent on the one piece of technology that was responsible for the end of civilization.

It said 9:14 a.m.

Nick had the strange vertigo-like sensation, not knowing whether he was up early—going to bed at three-in-the-morning usually meant he was up closer to noon—or whether he'd pulled a rip-van-winkle and had skipped a day.

Nick stood up sharply. He and Jimmy were alone in the dark minus Jimmy's flashlight and their phones. "I knew this would happen," Jimmy said.

Nick didn't respond but, instead, reached for the penlight he'd placed on the cellar wall shelf three days earlier. He clicked it on, not really shining at anything in particular, but using it for the ambient light it added to the room.

On the same shelf lay other items he and Jimmy had grabbed that first day: candles, all of the canned food from the house, and their dad's pistol, a Springfield XD9. It was a nine-millimeter, and it looked brand new, shiny black. It wasn't new, Nick understood, just barely used. He still remembered when his dad had gotten it—right before Jimmy and his stepmother came along.

Nick's dad had said it was for home protection. And after he took Nick to the range a couple of times—twelve is pretty young to shoot a pistol in that caliber, but Nick was always big for his age—Nick's dad had put the handgun in one of those quick-access vaults beside the bed and left it.

Quick-access—it even said that on the side of the vault—was an oxymoron. Nick and Jimmy had spent an eternity trying to get inside it. It had been an obvious reaction; after hearing and then seeing the violence that was breaking out, they had believed it was just a matter of time before they had to defend themselves. They felt like idiots after they realized the key code their dad had set was ONE, TWO, THREE, FOUR.

Some of that sense, the need to defend themselves from impending doom, had abated in the last three days. Now, they knew that the crazies didn't come knocking on your door. They had to see or hear you. You had to do something to get their attention. Then it was blind rage and hatred that was unleashed upon you, like the DataMind app hadn't ever helped people deal with stress or aggression in the first place but had, instead, bottled it up for later. It was a less comical version of Serenity Now, the joke from Nick's dad's favorite show, *Seinfeld*.

Nick stroked the Springfield, still in its holster, and admired the two magazines and half-empty box of ammo beside it.

"What are we going to do?" Jimmy asked.
"Right now?"

"Yeah, right now," Jimmy said sounding even more squirmy.

"Right now, I'm going to pee."

Jimmy exhaled in frustration, and Nick walked clumsily to the door. Against the corner stood the old Stevens single-shot sixteen-gauge. He grabbed it, opened the breach to make sure it was loaded, and snapped it back together. He didn't pull back the hammer. He didn't expect to use it. Not if their luck held out.

"Be back in a second."

"Here. Take this with you," Jimmy said handing him a two-liter bottle filled with his own urine.

Now it was Nick's turn to exhale in frustration. He threw the sling of the Stevens shotgun over his shoulder, grabbed the two-liter, grabbed the roll of toilet paper hung on a nail on the wall, and headed out the door quietly.

This was always Nick's least favorite part of the routine. Anytime he or Jimmy were outside was a precarious situation. Danger was always right around the corner, literally. But coming up the steps from the basement was his least favorite part. He had no way of looking out or listening before opening the basement door. There was no window to peek out of. For all he knew, some crazy could be crouched down, sleeping at the bottom landing of the stairs. *Do they sleep?* Nick wondered. He didn't know the answer. It was always

40

stupid stuff like this that crowded his mind, grabbed for his attention when he ought to be focusing on his surroundings.

He stopped after climbing three or four stairs, right when his head was about to pop up over the top and he could see out onto the street. He listened. The wind blew in intermittent gusts, making scrapes and scratches against the street and sidewalk with paper and other litter. How quickly Nick had learned the difference between these sounds and real crazy activity.

He headed up and over, not stopping at the top to check his surroundings. Once you were exposed, the important thing was limiting how long you were out there. Get it over with, was what he told himself.

He turned his back on the street and passed through the alleyway between the house and the garage, leading to the small backyard. Besides being inside, this was the safest place to be, Nick believed. The small backyard—his dad hated to mow—was enclosed with tall evergreen shrubs. His dad had told him they were impenetrable, the kind that were grown in parts of Europe as hedgerows that unintentionally stopped tanks. That wasn't why Nick's dad had grown them. It wasn't his dad's choice at all; it was Grandpa Joe who had planted them long before Nick was born. And here they were, thick, mangled, out-of-control wild and alive. Nothing about the last three days had fazed these shrubs. They made him feel safe, not just from the cover they provided while he relieved himself boy-scout style but from their intrinsic strength. *Who knows?* Nick thought. *Maybe I'm going crazy too. When did I become an animist?*

Nick did his business in a little hole dug with the shovel they had left in the corner of the yard on the first day. He poured in the contents of the two-liter. It made a disgusting soup which he quickly covered back up. These micro latrines he and his brother had been digging had marked up a surprising amount of the backyard, like giant moles or groundhogs systematically destroying someone's greenery.

He leaned the shovel back up against the hedge. He did so carefully. Another quickly learned skill was taking care with anything that could fall, anything that could make noise and draw attention. He looked at the shovel head. He could see the beginnings of a light bead of rust starting to form. His dad would have killed them for leaving this tool out in the rain to rust. Nick chuckled at the insanity of his idea: *now my Dad would kill us just because he went broke.*

Nick edged to the other side of the backyard to a corner between the hedgerow and back of the house. From this corner there was a gap allowing him to spy on the road with little chance of being spotted. He pressed his head against the gap until he felt some of the oversized thorns threaten to poke him. He waited and watched. He looked at the power poles that, until hours ago, had carried kilowatts of electricity through the city. Now what were they? Fossils, he figured. Something his descendants, if he lived that long, would have trouble believing in. The story of invisible power traveling through these poles and lines would seem more incomprehensible than the building of the pyramids or Stonehenge. And eventually the poles would rot and the lines on the ground would slowly get covered with grass and dirt. If mankind ever rebuilt, centuries from now, they would one day discover these strange formations during archeological digs: asphalt roads and wires. It wouldn't make sense. Too many of the pieces of the puzzle would have been removed for anyone to understand what they were for, or so Nick believed.

The other houses across the street didn't look that different. If anyone was still alive there, anyone unaffected by the update, they wouldn't have their lights on or be making a commotion anyway. Electricity had become a secret commodity, something to be used and enjoyed in one's most inner sanctum. For the boys, it had been the basement. He was sure Mrs. Lambert, before she lost her marbles and her life, probably had some closet or bedroom with blacked out windows. Some place she watched old home videos, looked at all the people she'd lost forever. No wonder she lost it, he thought.

He could see part of Mrs. Lambert's house. When the wind blew, it moved her still opened front door, making it squeak. He had gotten pretty good at blotting out unpleasant memories; like a gag reflex, they came upon him quickly, and he had to fight them back down before he spewed.

What happened to Mrs. Lambert was worth remembering, Nick decided. Not the gory details. But the reality that there were still crazies out there, and even though they had avoided them, hadn't been attacked—it didn't mean that it wouldn't happen, that it couldn't happen to them. Just because you don't see them doesn't mean they aren't there. They are. Over a half-million of them in the state of Alaska alone. Tens of thousands in Fairbanks.

He had figured by what he'd seen on the news before it went down, what he'd seen on the street, and what he'd heard on shortwave that the crazies weren't capable of taking care of themselves any longer, at least not beyond eating some scraps out of the garbage or drinking water from a puddle. Most of the time, they were dormant, slowly roaming the streets until they were provoked—an easy task. They attacked anyone and everyone including other people affected by the update, though they seemed to preferentially go after the unaffected. Nick, in his mental plan-to-survive-the-apocalypse version-1.0, had hoped that the crazies would wear themselves out quickly, that it was a game of attrition, and that if he and his brother just stayed-put, eventually there wouldn't be any crazies left.

He still might be right, but the lights going out added to the reality that they were going into the deep end, that this was for real stakes. Even more worrisome to Nick was their food supply, or lack thereof. His stomach growled just thinking about it. How were they supposed to go restock their supplies without getting attacked? Going to the supermarket downtown seemed like suicide. He thought about checking out their next-door neighbors' pantries, but all the extra noise involved in breaking into locked homes would be just as dangerous as waltzing downtown. There were no easy answers.

CHAPTER 5

WHEN NICK RETURNED to the basement, it looked like a different place entirely. Jimmy, a regular Martha Stewart, had lit all the candles and carefully placed them around the room for proper fengshui.

"What are you thinking?" Nick said more than asked as he went to several of the candles and blew them out.

"Hey, what are you doing?" Jimmy shrieked.

"Thanks for inviting me to a romantic candle-lit dinner, but I don't think this is the time or place for it, Nancy." He caught himself too late. He knew Jimmy hated that nickname and it would only invite trouble. But Jimmy had made his bed and would have to lie in it, Nick told himself.

"The lights are out. What are we supposed to do?" Jimmy asked.

"How about conserving our precious resources, for starters?"

Jimmy had that dumb look on his face, the one that Nick had seen a hundred times. It wasn't the look of genuine stupidity; it was the one he wore before he started getting really mad.

"While you were out for a stroll, I had to make decisions," Jimmy said. "And I, for one, don't want to live down here like some rat in the dark."

"Calm down," Nick countered.

"No. You came in here guns blazing. You made all the hot-headed decisions, blowing out the candles I lit. You're the one acting hastily. How about you try to slow down and talk to me before you go behind me and change what I've done."

The two boys were face to face, looking like they were about to shove each other. It was mostly Jimmy who presented the aggressive signs. Nick realized what was going on, that he needed to diffuse Jimmy before things got worse. But at the same time, he didn't want to back down.

Jimmy spun off toward some of the smoldering, snuffed out candles on the wall shelves. He carefully, as if he dared Nick to defy him, lit half of the candles that were out.

That was Jimmy's pattern. As wimpy as he seemed to Nick, he did have a level of aggression, a push-back impulse. But he wasn't brave. He was more inclined to regain part of what he lost, some mental compromise he'd made with himself. That as long as he got some back, some portion of whatever was taken from him—he could live with that. Nick thought it was pathetic. But he also knew that if he pushed Jimmy's buttons further that there was an even more childish, ridiculous version of his brother waiting to come out.

"Now, we can see each other," Jimmy said.

"Look, we need to talk for real," Nick said.

"I tried earlier. You just talk with me when it's convenient for you. When are you going to listen to me? I mean, I know I'm your younger brother. But you're not that much older than me. Give me some credit."

Nick had to hold his tongue. What he felt like saying and doing would only make things worse. "You're right. I'm sorry." He almost couldn't believe the words coming out his mouth.

Jimmy made a different face, like he was ready to listen but wasn't convinced Nick was sincere.

Nick went on. "The lights going out doesn't change things that much. I mean, it makes things suck down here. I'll give you that. But we're not in more physical danger than we were yesterday. If anything— the way I see it—the crazies are killing each other. So, each day there are fewer of them out there to face."

"You think we should just carry on? Stay calm and starve to death?"

"I didn't say that," Nick answered. "I'm just saying the power going out doesn't necessarily mean we have to change plans. But food is a concern of mine."

"So, let's go to Deadhorse then." Jimmy's voice changed. The very mention of Deadhorse made him sound ten years younger, like a kid wanting to go to Disneyland.

It took every fiber of Nick's inner-being to keep from smashing this weak, childish side of Jimmy. He hated it. Not just because it was annoying. There was something else about it. If they weren't riding out the end of the world together, he would have relished delivering a snarky blow to his brother's ego.

"Slow down," Nick said. "Let's deal with things one at a time. You'd agree—I think—that the biggest risk to our future, besides crazies, is food." Nick waited for Jimmy to affirm.

"Yeah, but…"

"Then the first thing to figure out is how to find something to eat, a way that doesn't involve running into crazies."

Jimmy nodded his head sheepishly. Nick knew if you mentioned enough crazies and the idea of being attacked, Jimmy would cower a little.

"The way I figure, the grocery store is out," Nick continued. "It's in a busy part of town and it's too big. Too easy to run into crazies. But what if we case a house, determine it's empty, and rob their pantry?"

"What? Are you serious? That sounds like a terrible idea," Jimmy said impulsively. "You think sitting outside, exposed all day while we watch a neighbor's house to be sure it's empty is less risky than quickly going to the store and back? We might as well go to Deadhorse."

Nick ignored that last part. "We don't have to sit outside to do it. We have a perfectly good house above us we can spy from."

"But you said it wasn't safe up there. That the basement was the only place we should stay."

"That was before we ran out of food, little brother."

He could tell Jimmy didn't like it, but he was starting to budge. He was going to cave-in to Nick's plan—he knew it. It wasn't that they were completely out of food. But the diminishing supply and—just as importantly—the dwindling options had already hampered their appetites, enough to recognize what was coming if they didn't find more supplies.

"Well, maybe. But what do we do in three weeks after all our neighbors' food is gone? We can't…" Jimmy startled. His head jerked as he squinted in the dim light towards their containers of food and water on the shelf on the far wall. "Nick, what about water? How long will the water run?"

50

Nick hadn't even thought of water. He scrambled to come up with a quick-fix answer, some way to maintain his high-ground and appear to have all the answers.

"We've experienced power outages before," Nick said. "The pump station maintains pressure even when our house loses power."

"Yeah, but they'll lose power too at some point. If they haven't already."

"Then we'll fill up all the bathtubs and sinks."

"Eww! No way am I going to drink water from where you washed your butt—"

"We don't have to do that if it snows," Nick interrupted. "It won't be that long before it starts snowing again. Then we'll have an endless supply of water right outside our door."

Jimmy shook his head. "This is getting ridiculous, Nick. We can't…I can't live like this. You know how cold it gets here after the snow starts falling. Even in the basement. I can't do it."

"Alright, then," Nick said sounding a bit perturbed. "Let's hear your solution."

"You already know what I want. Deadhorse."

"And how are we going to do that? And don't just tell me we're going to drive there. If you can't think through more of the logistics than that, then I don't want to hear it."

"I don't know how," Jimmy said. "But just think of it. We'd be miles from here. Miles from trouble. Bob said he had generators and food to last for years. And he's Grandpa Joe's friend. He might as well be extended family. As far as we know, he's our last living relative."

"That's it? That's all you got?" Nick asked with obvious insincerity. His patience for Jimmy was running thin.

"Yeah, that's it. I described the most stable, safe place to be, and you ask me if *that's all*."

"Then why don't we go to Fiji while we're at it? Or Boca Raton? I hear it's beautiful this time of year."

"Shut up. You know this is different."

"I don't know it's different. Deadhorse is over four hundred miles from here. And given our present situation, it might as well be two million miles."

"So, you'd rather live here like two rats in the gutter? That's your plan, big brother?" Jimmy was holding his hands on his hips. Nick hated that gesture.

"Yeah, Nancy. That's right. I plan to live. Did you catch that? There were two parts. I *plan*." He drew the word out sarcastically. "That means I actually think about what I want and how to get it. And I plan to live. You don't seem to care about either."

"I care *how* we live," Jimmy said with a higher tone.

"No, that's not it at all. You just want to be comfortable. You want out of a jam because you don't like it. You don't want to go to Deadhorse because that's what's best, you want to go because you think it's some panacea, some mirage that if you were to get there—and we wouldn't. We'd die trying—you'd realize it was just as crappy as this place. The whole world went broke, Jimmy. Get it through your thick head. This isn't a fantasy land. This is reality."

Jimmy stood there steaming. Nick knew what was happening, but he didn't care. Jimmy was short circuiting. Nick had seen it a hundred times. There was no use trying to prevent it now. It was going to happen eventually anyway. *Who knows?* Nick thought. *Maybe this will be good for him. Maybe he'll snap out of it and grow up.*

"So that's it?" Jimmy asked with tears welling up.

"Yeah, Nancy. That's it."

"Nothing I can do or say?"

"No, there's not. Some things aren't up to you. We're not going anywhere. We're staying right here until I see there's good reason to move. You're not in charge around here. I am."

Jimmy sunk into himself, almost expressionless. Nick knew there were two ways it could go from this point forward. Either Jimmy would implode or explode. He hoped for both of their sakes it wasn't the latter.

Jimmy seemed to take a labored breath in, then he moved past Nick, brushing against his shoulder. "Where do you think you're going?" Nick demanded as Jimmy reached the door.

"You're not the only one that needs to pee," Jimmy said. On another day, that response would have been met with a smile from both of the boys. Today it was a surreal, emotionless, lifeless expression. What wasn't said was louder than what was. Nick wondered if he'd ever see his brother again. But he wasn't about to apologize.

"Don't forget the Stevens," Nick said.

Jimmy had a slightly confused look. Obviously, Nick's words didn't compute. Nick nodded towards the shotgun behind Jimmy. Jimmy grabbed it almost begrudgingly.

"And Jimmy…"

Jimmy looked at his brother with the tiniest inkling of hope in his eyes, like a dog waiting for a crumb from its master's table.

"Don't get us both killed. Keep it down, will ya?"

CHAPTER 6

MINUTES LATER JIMMY returned, and the rest of the day was as Nick had predicted. Once Jimmy started down his spiral, there was nothing you could do for him. You certainly couldn't pull him back up the slide. If there was any strategy to it all, Nick decided, it was to try to speed up the process, try to get Jimmy down and out of the doldrums. Nick figured it was like catching the flu. You could buy all the over-the-counter medicine the store had, but, in the end, the virus had to run its course. Simple as that. Nothing else to do but get through it. That fever was there to kill the virus and jamming handfuls of Tylenol down your throat only delayed your agony. That was Nick's theory. Only time would tell if he was right.

Nick left the basement, deciding to fly solo and leave Jimmy sitting in the dark. Nick knew there were things to do besides moping around feeling sorry for himself. He didn't understand his brother. He recognized all his quirks, could even diagnose some of the reasons why he'd ended up that way. But ultimately, he just couldn't really empathize. Why expect life to be nice to you? Why wait around bellyaching about how things didn't go your way? You weren't entitled to a darn thing in this world. If Nick wasn't sure of that before the update, he was now.

Inside their house, Nick moved from room to room with new eyes. This place didn't look like the home he remembered. It was full of artifacts, things from a bygone era. Joy dish soap, a Keurig coffee maker, a Wi-Fi router—all useless items to him now.

After filling up all the bathtubs and sinks with water, Nick looked through the house for any items of food that he and Jimmy had missed on their initial pass through the house three days ago. He looked inside the refrigerator hoping to find some cheese or lunch meat in a drawer. But the only things left were some outdated yogurt and leftover meatloaf his mom had made almost two weeks ago. His nose told him what his brain should have: foods go bad with or without refrigeration.

At this point, Nick had no more reason to be in the house. It wasn't that dangerous, not like being outside in plain view. But he knew it was more likely for him to be seen or heard up there than down in the basement. Still, he didn't want to go back down into that dungeon, now more of a torture chamber than a retreat with Jimmy's insufferable drama. Nick couldn't stand it, and he didn't know why.

To an outsider, Jimmy wasn't that bad. All his teachers and guidance counselors had thought he had a lot of potential. They had felt that with the right attention, the right therapy, and the giant horse-pill Jimmy swallowed on a daily basis, he had a chance to be someone special. Their parents had been concerned when Jimmy first started the doom-and-gloom routine, but in the end, they bought him his antidepressants and forgot about it. They, like all the other working age professionals around them, were working more hours per day than they ever had in their entire lives. The DataMind app had done that to them all. Highly focused, over-achieving, dollar-centric workaholics. The whole lot of them. But that's the problem with mass movements. It doesn't leave anyone to dissent. No contrary points of view. Nick and Jimmy's parents, their friends' parents, all of their teachers—everybody over the age of eighteen and under sixty was addicted to the high of success.

So, in that sense, Jimmy was a pre-update casualty of DataMind. Probably one of thousands. But now, anyone alive was a victim, or at least could see themselves that way. Nick could see that Jimmy could have used more help, that he hadn't adapted to their parents' marriage as well as Nick had. Maybe it wasn't fair to compare himself to his younger brother.

Jimmy's real dad had died when Jimmy was four, so there was that. Maybe the damage was done. Maybe that's the kind of thing that does it to a kid. But Nick was certain there were people—successful people and long before the appearance of DataMind—who had grown up in harder spots than that and had come out the other side on top of life. They made it. Why couldn't Jimmy?

After stalling for as long as he could stomach it, Nick ran out of rationalizations and went back down into the basement. It was getting late in the p.m., but the boys had many hours of night left before they would naturally get sleepy. Nick had planned for this, grabbing the melatonin bottle he found by his stepmother's bedside table. With any luck he could shut off the world, and maybe tomorrow Jimmy would have completed his mope-about exercises. Maybe they could get back to living life.

Even with the low light of the one candle Jimmy had burning and the glow from Jimmy listening to music on his phone, Nick wasn't feeling the effects of the melatonin. He should be, but it was that nagging impulse to jump up, grab Jimmy's phone out of his hands, and lecture him about how foolish and wasteful he was using it, to listen to music when there would be no easy way to recharge it. Their phones, Nick realized, were the true artifacts, the relics from a lost time. Nick planned to use his battery life sparingly. He had pictures of his parents, his friends on his phone—all things he would never see again. And he wasn't about to squander those by 'getting his jam on' as Jimmy liked to say when he was in a joking mood.

Something else nagged at him, something he couldn't clearly articulate. He experienced it as a general sense of anxiety, and now the melatonin was starting to kick in ushering in the beginning of the race between his subconscious and his physiology—the former trying to surface the source of his unseen concern, the latter letting the sandman into the room. Can't be that important, Nick thought, as his eyes closed. I'll figure it out in the morning.

CHAPTER 7

MORNING NEVER CAME. Not like Nick had planned, anyway. Long before the update, the boys had moved their wake-up time closer and closer to noon, and now that there was no bedroom window with screaming sunshine to wake them, there circadian rhythm was on a forward slant, waking up later and later, losing another slice of the day until someday they would have slept through an entire working day and would have to endure the vampire routine.

But these weren't the thoughts in Nick's mind as his consciousness swam to the surface for air. Instead, there was a general alarm off in his head, knowing something wasn't right. He was hoping he was just having a bad dream. Heaven knew he'd had plenty of those lately.

He gasped air as if he'd been holding his breath all night. Eyes open, the room was completely dark. The candle had burned out sometime while he was asleep, and apparently, Jimmy wasn't still getting his jam on. He thought about turning over and going back to sleep. A false alarm, he thought.

Then he heard it: a low unmistakable rumble.

A car. But not the sound of a motorist passing by erratically as they had on the first day after the update. This was the sound of an idling vehicle.

Nick's body responded before his mind was even sure what was happening. He stood up in the darkness, groped for his blue jeans and thrust his legs and feet through. His mind, still playing catch-up, had the sense to turn on his penlight, the one clipped to his t-shirt collar.

Although the little light seemed piercingly bright, it shined little light on the situation. Except for one thing: Jimmy was gone.

As Nick scrambled toward the door, he did a one-eighty. His feet almost slipped out from under him as he pounced on the Springfield nine-millimeter. He shoved one magazine into his pants pocket, slammed the other into the pistol. He didn't know why, but he grabbed the half-empty box of rounds and shoved them into his other pants pocket. He racked the pistol which *clanged* loudly in the dark room.

He'd played the part before, pantomiming this action, but this time it was real, and the sound of the gun's action slamming forward, cocking it, and turning it from an object of potential into one of deadly action was too real. His hand shook a little as he ran toward the door.

After stepping into tennis shoes with no socks, Nick went out the door, this time without any care for the sound. He wasn't the one making sound, but he had a pretty good idea who was.

At the top of the stairs, Nick tried to get his bearings. He was lightheaded from the quick acceleration up the staircase with a still half-sleeping heart.

Nothing outside looked amiss. And thankfully, he didn't see any crazies. Not yet, anyway.

The sound was coming from the garage, just like he'd suspected but was too afraid of being right to acknowledge. He grabbed the door to the garage to open it, but his hand slipped as he tried. Locked.

Confused, Nick grabbed at the keys about his neck.

Not having a holster for his pistol and needing both hands to sort out the keys, Nick hunched over and held his Springfield between his knees. A precarious position regardless, but Nick felt even more exposed knowing that at any moment some crazy would hear and catch wind of the commotion. They don't announce themselves or their intentions from what he'd seen. Besides a lunatic's battle cry, he wouldn't know they were there until it was probably too late.

He tried the wrong key, cursed himself for his stupid mistake, and then found the right one. The door opened. Nick let go of it, grabbed the keys, his gun, then shouldered his way into the garage.

Almost instantly, he began to cough from the exhaust fumes, but he didn't dare leave the door open. He slammed it shut and locked it. Then he turned and really looked at the situation for the first time. The lights were out here too, so Nick had to shine his pen light around the room. He found himself acting out his pantomime bit yet again: he held his flashlight underneath his gun the way he'd seen cops do it on TV.

If Jimmy's sleeping pad hadn't been empty, Nick would have worried that some crazy or even an unaffected person had broken into the garage and started up Grandpa Joe's old Dodge Ram hi-top conversion van, the kind that Nick had seen on the A-team reruns.

Instead, Nick knew to look for his brother. He wasn't in the driver's seat, and, although it was difficult to see through the smoke, Nick didn't see him standing around the van either. As he swept the room, he caught the first glimpse of his brother: feet lying on the ground sticking out from behind the van.

"Jimmy!" he yelled. There was no answer and no movement from his brother.

Bang! A pounding sound came from the garage door. Nick knew all too well what that was. He cursed himself again for not turning off the motor when he had first come in. *That's what I get for worrying about Jimmy,* he told himself. *And it's liable to be my last mistake.*

He rushed to his brother who was face up, unconscious with his head next to the exhaust pipe.

More bangs from the garage door. It sounded like more than one of them now.

"Jimmy, wake up!" Nick said while grabbing and shaking his brother like a ragdoll. He didn't know where his strength came from. Adrenaline, he guessed. He pulled Jimmy upright, up against the back of the van and continued shaking him. If he hadn't been unconscious to start with, the amount of head banging against the van door would have likely caused the condition.

Jimmy's neck and head were limp and hung grotesquely from his collar bone. The sight only angered Nick more and he shook and yelled at his brother for dear life.

Like he'd been a million miles away, Jimmy suddenly opened his eyes with the same level of confusion that Nick had experienced moments before. More so. "What? What's happening?" Jimmy said raising one hand to his head.

"There isn't time. Can you walk? Can you move?" Nick asked.

"Yeah, I think so."

More banging from the garage door. Jimmy stood upright, alert. "What's…"

"They're here," Nick said. "We gotta get out of here."

CHAPTER 8

MORE POUNDING CAME from the side door to the garage, the one that Nick had entered through. Nick knew it was only a matter of time before they kicked through that weaker door—he hoped they couldn't bust through the main garage door—or, if they had any brain cells left to think with, they might bust out the windows in the back and try to climb up and over.

"Come on," Nick demanded as he walked around the van.

"Where are we going?" Jimmy asked.

"Nowhere, just yet. Not until we load this van. Grab anything you think could be useful."

Jimmy started going to work, to Nick's surprise. Maybe he'd lost enough brain cells to be more agreeable, Nick thought. Then he squashed the notion, frustrated with himself for wasting time thinking about something other than getting out of the situation, preferably in one piece.

Both boys had pen lights on their lanyards. Jimmy's was brighter than Nick's and between the two lights they could just make their way through the boxes upon boxes of storage. Things that would ordinarily go in someone's attic if they didn't mind cannibalizing their garage. Still, the two lights weren't enough to see everything. Not before the crazies would break through.

Nick had an idea. He moved to the driver's side door and opened it. Jimmy saw him and followed after. "Shouldn't we turn off the engine? It's getting really hard to see…" He coughed. "Or breathe in here."

Nick looked at Jimmy's face for as long as he could, as long as the banging from the door would allow him to. He watched for some crack in the façade, a sign of a joke, some smirk to indicate Jimmy knew how ridiculous his statement was. Nothing. No gesture demonstrating the awareness that it was he who had created this situation and that the time to have turned the engine off was twenty minutes ago.

"We've got bigger problems now," Nick finally answered.

The cab faced away from the garage door. Nick would have traded all his football trophies, his first kiss, and his big toe to have it facing the other direction.

Nick reached beneath the steering column, groping for an object he didn't know he would recognize if he found it. He pulled something, a knob. A soft *pop* sound came from outside the van. It was barely even audible against the roar of thuds and thumps now coming from multiple spots on both the garage door and the side door.

"That's for the gas," Jimmy yelled from the other side of the van. Then Nick realized he had pulled the button that opened the lid to the fuel tank.

I've got to be getting close, he told himself. Then to the left of the wheel, higher up, he found a small, smooth, circular tab. He pulled it, and the forward high beams shined brilliantly, causing him to wince from the brightness.

Once his eyes adjusted to the new levels, he could easily make out objects in the garage just through ambient light. He looked at the side door, the one he was most concerned about becoming the first point of failure. Propped up to the right of the door was the Stevens shotgun Jimmy had brought upstairs with him.

"Jimmy, get your gun," he said pointing.

Nick moved on to grabbing fuel cans, some automotive fluids, some flashlights that probably didn't work, and tossing them into the back of the van. Out of the corner of his eye, he saw Jimmy approach the shotgun. He acted like a scared little kid who had been ordered by his parents to enter a dark room. He even saw a micro-expression, a momentary wavering of resolve like Jimmy wanted to turn back and admit he was scared of the pounding. Instead, he crept forward toward the gun but with his eyes glued to the door. Then, when he was close enough, he darted for it and sprang back toward the van.

Jimmy began to put it in the van with the other things. "No, put it over your shoulder and keep packing," Nick instructed.

Jimmy started on a tower of boxes as if he was going to either go through the boxes to determine their contents or blindly grab them and put them in the van. "Don't waste time on those," Nick said. "Look, in the corner. Get that spare tire and gear."

Again, Jimmy followed his brother's instructions. Nick scanned the room for something he'd missed. He didn't know what, but he had that itch like it was right under his nose. He knew, if they made it, this was the last time he'd ever see this garage, his last chance to bring anything from his former life with him into the next.

A different sound from the side door. Not just the thumps and screams, but a higher pitched crack. Before he got around the van to lay eyes on it, Nick knew that was a bad sign.

Jimmy and Nick ran into each other in their haste, causing the full-sized spare tire to be dropped and bounce and roll to the garage door.

"Get that tire into the van and get ready," Nick said. Whatever that meant.

Nick rushed the side door. There was a definite crack forming. And with each impact from the other side, the crack grew longer, threatening to run the length of the door.

Nick froze for a second; his mind didn't want to provide the answer. He was usually quick on his feet, a quality that gave him confidence. But in this moment, nothing surfaced. *How do you fix a door that's breaking?* He even scanned the workbench along the side wall for a two-by-four and nails, something like how he'd seen people board up windows in corny zombie movies.

The crack expanded exponentially, and Nick saw the door begin to open. He slammed his body against it, forcing it shut.

"That's it, Jimmy! They're getting through," he yelled. Nick didn't recognize the sound of his own voice; it was too wild, too desperate sounding.

"What do I do?" Jimmy asked.

"Just get in the van and be ready."

"Ready for what?" Jimmy pleaded.

Nick didn't have time to go through it all. "Look, just get in. Lock all the doors except for the sliding side door. Leave it open just enough for me to squeeze through."

"Then what?"

"Then nothing. Do what I'm telling you!" Nick yelled through clenched teeth. The door behind him felt elastic, and each pulse, each impact behind him sent a wave through him that he had to ride. Physically, he couldn't hang on much longer; his legs were starting to shake from the strain, and he knew even if his body lasted, soon the door itself would break.

Nick watched in glances he cast between the pulses, between times that he had his whole mind and will focused on holding back the deluge. During each wave, he felt the Springfield XD9 tucked into his waistband dig a little deeper into his back. He saw Jimmy faithfully carry out his instructions locking each door from the inside manually. When he was done, Jimmy gave his brother a thumbs up from within the cab. Nick wished he'd get out of the driver's seat. Jimmy wasn't going to do the driving, but Nick figured if this was going to work there would be a moment to shift positions.

Now it was time. Time to take action and enact the plan, his plan. But none of this was really his plan. His mind wandered from blaming Jimmy for all of this, to his parents and what they'd think of it, and finally to whether they would survive. Ultimately, Nick realized he was stalling. The time for thinking was over. He needed to pull the trigger and let the chips fall.

He rode one last wave with the pulsing door, opened his eyes, and sprinted toward the unlocked door of the van. He couldn't tell, but he hoped Jimmy had left it open enough for him to enter.

Coming from behind him, Nick heard the door collapse and the crazies punch through. Then as he nearly slipped turning the corner of the back of the van, he heard the hoops, hollers, and footsteps of the angry mob enter the garage.

"Get out of the driver's seat," he told Jimmy as he squeezed through the gap in the sliding door. Immediately, he turned and pulled the door shut as fast and as hard as he could. The door slammed but didn't make the metallic sound it normally would. Instead, there was a dull thump and the accompanying shriek of the crazy who lost part of a finger in the door.

Nick pushed down the door lock and retreated back from the door and jumped to the driver's seat. Jimmy was in the back now, and the whole van reverberated with the metallic clangs of the crazies pounding away at them.

"Hold onto something," Nick told Jimmy.

Nick found the same knob he'd groped in the dark for and pushed it, turning off the high beams.

"Why'd you do that?" Jimmy begged.

Nick didn't answer. But he knew why: just because these people went broke and were crazy didn't mean they had superpowers. They couldn't see any better in the dark than the two of them could. The boys just needed time. A few extra seconds even.

Nick jolted as there was a smack against his side window. So much for total confusion, he thought. One more direct punch might shatter the glass.

Nick pulled the automatic transmission shifter down one click. He couldn't see, but he hoped this was like every other car he'd ever driven and that he'd shifted into Reverse. *No way to tell except to…*

He floored the accelerator and the van moved the several feet between it and the garage door. Nick felt momentarily weightless as he imagined the crazies were being shaken free of the vehicle. But then a dent in his plan emerged as the van smashed into the garage door and refused to burst through.

Nick did the only thing he could think to do. After all, all his eggs were in this basket. If it didn't work…

He pushed the shifter down two notches counting consciously until he thought it was in Drive. Then he accelerated forward but less forcefully than before.

The van lunged forward. Nick heard mixed sounds: something metallic clanging on the concrete floor—he figured it was a piece of the van, a bumper maybe—and the moans and squalls of crazies that had been caught in the van's path.

When he imagined he was back where he'd started, he threw the shifter up two and slammed the gas pedal again. This time the impact with the garage door yielded more fruit. The van lodged into it, stuck like before. But there was daylight breaking through the cracks in the door.

Progress, Nick told himself. But at a cost. The new light inside the garage made it possible for the remaining crazies—there had to be over ten—to attack the van with more accuracy.

A rear side-window crashed and Jimmy nearly fell down in panic trying to get away from it.

"Hold on," Nick reassured him.

Nick moved the van forward again, told himself it was going to work this time. He put his foot down screeching the tires.

This time it did work. The garage door came off at its hinges, collapsing on top of the van.

As Nick backed out to the street, he whipped the steering wheel, threw the shifter into drive, and stomped the pedal once again. The garage door fell behind them in the street.

He looked in the rear-view mirror as several crazies chased them like stray dogs. But it was useless. He was already up to forty-five mph, and they, as crazy as they were, quickly realized their futility.

What he saw next shouldn't have surprised him, not after what he'd seen at Mrs. Lambert's house. As soon as the crazies' fever-pitched minds abandoned their original target, they turned and unflinchingly attacked each other.

Nick slowed around a curve in the road and lost sight of the whole scene.

"We made it," Jimmy said.

"Yeah, well." Nick didn't know what to say. And he wasn't sure how Jimmy could be the least bit happy or excited. They had just passed within an inch of their lives. He figured it was because Jimmy didn't have to do anything. He'd been saved in the truest since of the word. But instead of expressing gratitude or thanks, he wore his goofy grin like they'd just gotten off the Space Mountain ride.

Relief and happiness were similar enough to get them confused, Nick figured, trying to cut Jimmy some slack. He was the only family Nick had. Despite how stupid and selfish he acted, Jimmy was it.

Clang!

"What was that?" Jimmy asked, instantly losing all positive inertia.

Nick didn't answer but checked all his mirrors for assailants. Nothing.

Clang. Clang.

This wasn't some gravel thrown up under the car, it was something intentional. And it came from on top of the van.

CHAPTER 9

"BRACE YOURSELF," Nick commanded.

"What are you going to do?" Jimmy asked as he grabbed the hand grip above the sliding side door.

"No, that's not going to do it. Sit down, and buckle your seatbelt," Nick said, not really answering his question.

More clangs and thumps came from above. Nick even looked up reflexively, although he knew he couldn't see through the ceiling. Nick realized the crazy must have held onto the luggage rack on top. He couldn't believe this punk didn't fall off with the garage door. Going broke didn't make you super strong, Nick told himself. But whatever power you get through psychotic levels of rage and motivation—they had it.

Nick looked at the rear-view mirror, making sure Jimmy was buckled up. Then he stomped the accelerator as more clangs rang out above. The crazy was moving closer to the front of the van, making its way toward the windshield, Nick thought.

Nick was surprised—although he shouldn't have been—that punching the accelerator didn't cause the van to spin its tires and lunge forward like before. The difference was he was already going fifty-five mph and the old V-8 was all low-end torque. It just didn't have the top-end power that even Nick's dad's little Honda Civic had.

The van, like a begrudging laborer, followed Nick's instructions and accelerated up to eighty-five mph. Nick felt the van shudder and shake, and he knew that was all she had in her.

"Here we go," he warned.

Then he stomped on the brakes with two feet. The van did an S-shape, swerving a bit as its disk-brakes' pads demonstrated their uneven wear. Before the van came to a complete stop, the crazy that had held on so tenaciously before flew forward, first bouncing over the windshield and hood, then flopping onto the hard pavement in front of the vehicle.

Nick, with two hands squeezing at ten-and-two o'clock, stared over the steering wheel at the body in the road, watching it for movement.

"What are you waiting for?" Jimmy pleaded. "Let's get out of here."

Nick said nothing. He just stared. He didn't even know what he was waiting on. *The danger had passed, and the crazy was off of them. It was over.* That's what his conscious mind told him, but somehow, for some unknown reason he waited.

Only later did he know what this hidden part of himself was doing. It was the same part that he had used on the field playing football. It was what he'd discovered a couple of summers ago. If he paid attention and didn't think too hard, he could sense when he, the quarterback, was about to be rushed by the defensive linemen. He'd tried to understand where this spidey-sense had come from. The best he'd come up with was after his Intro to Psychology course he took at James Madison High School. He'd decided it was his subconscious calculating, processing, and making decisions about his surroundings, about the complex data that the computer part of his brain couldn't handle.

Ever since then, he'd learned to trust this instinct, and it hadn't let him down yet. But it was a bit unnerving knowing you were about to do something and not know what it was.

Then it all came together. The crazy on the road moved her leg. At first it was a tremor, something a newly dead or dying body could do through autonomic nervous response. But then the crazy slowly pulled her arms and hands up from her waist and tried to push herself off the road. She was wearing a white blouse over a short black skirt. Her shoes were long gone, probably before the garage, Nick thought.

Nick watched as the badly hurt woman stood up slowly with her back facing the van. Nick could see a dark, wine red stain seeping through the left side of the blouse. The crazy tried to straighten its back, but something caught internally and the once thirty-something brunette hunched back over.

Before she turned to face them and before he even knew what he was doing, Nick stepped on the gas. The old van sounded its monstrous roar, the result of both its massive big-block engine and its rusted-out muffler and exhaust pipe. The Dodge Ram lived up to its name, hitting the crazy and dragging her body for several yards before finally swallowing her up, making her disappear below its underbelly.

"Why'd you do that?" Jimmy asked.

This time Nick felt like answering. "I wanted to finish what I'd started." He paused, then corrected himself. "...what *it* started."

The boys were quiet for several minutes as the gravity of their experience settled in.

Nick drove. Nowhere in particular. Nowhere consciously. But after ten minutes he became aware of his self-made pattern: he was driving in a giant circle around Fairbanks using streets that had the least number of parked cars, which meant he was mostly using suburban routes around town.

Fairbanks was like that; it was Alaska's second biggest city, but you could only dress up the town so much. Winter was always coming, and people pretty much forgot all about pretense when the first cold chill smacked them in the face. Then it was a matter of survival. And the suburbs, just like Nick and Jimmy's neighborhood, was a comfortable solution for so many.

Nick kept his speed up. Twice they saw crazies roaming randomly down a street, but they were past them before they seemed to notice the target on wheels. More times than they could count, they would see in the rear-view mirror crazies run out onto the street and chase their van. As long as they kept driving, there was no chance they'd be caught, but it was unnerving. Nick felt like he was in a shark cage—out of danger but too close to ever feel safe.

Jimmy moved into the front passenger seat and started to buckle his seatbelt.

"You expect to get into a head-on collision?" Nick jeered.

Jimmy stopped short of buckling his belt. "Old habits, I guess." He let go of the belt, and it whipped back into place. "Nick, how much gas do we have?"

Now he wants to think ahead. "Half a tank," Nick answered.

"But how much is that? Five gallons? Ten?"

Nick didn't like the way Jimmy did this. He'd seen it before. It was frustrating how predictable

Jimmy was, yet how impossible to thwart. Jimmy had developed these mechanisms, or social tics as Nick called them. Just like his shut-down depressive act. It was all for manipulation, as far as Nick could tell. And this was no different. Jimmy liked to ask questions he knew you didn't know the answer to. To get you off-balance. To admit you weren't totally in control. Then he'd vie for influence.

"What does it matter?" Nick bashed back.

"Well, I think it matters quite a bit. As far as I can tell, the only thing keeping us out of reach from those crazies is this gas engine. If we run down to empty, we're sitting ducks."

"You think?" Nick said sarcastically.

"Come on. We don't have time for this," Jimmy insisted.

That was it. That was the button Nick was waiting to have pushed.

"*We* don't have time for this?" Nick echoed. "Since when were *we* making decisions? When did you last think about someone other than yourself?"

"I'm trying to find a way out for both of us," Jimmy said as innocently as he could.

"Why start now?"

"What's that supposed to mean?"

"Are you kidding me? Are you really asking me—"

"You're the one making all the decisions, deciding we were going to stay in Fairbanks indefinitely," Jimmy whined.

"And why did I have to make that choice for both of *us*?"

"You didn't. And it was the wrong choice anyways."

"We won't know that, Jimmy. Because now, we don't have the option to stay put. Thanks to you."

"What'd I do?"

Here was the classic Jimmy-moment: play dumb, invite someone to roll over you, then pull the victim-act.

"It's not going to work. Not this time, Jimmy. You forced my hand. You took away my choice, so, I guess, you won in that sense. But I'm not going to let you get away with pretending this isn't all your fault. You're a total screw-up. A screw-up by choice on top of it. No one made you lay down in the garage. No one made you start up the van and attract every crazy in earshot. Don't you dare act like you were so desperate you had no other options."

Jimmy jumped into the fray. "What? Now I didn't try to kill myself correctly? Let's add that to the list, shall we? How many things my little brother screwed up. Could you just once be concerned about me?"

"You haven't earned that. You used up people's sympathy a long time ago. Even Mom and Dad stopped caring years ago."

"That's not fair. You know they changed with the app."

Nick knew Jimmy was right; the superhuman drive for work and efficiency brought about by DataMind hadn't turned people into the best parents. If anything, it was the opposite. There are no such things as efficient relationships. But facts weren't important right now. What mattered was that Jimmy was held to account for the jam he'd put both of them in.

"Whatever makes you sleep better at night," Nick said. "I'm just saying, if not getting your way about Deadhorse was such a big deal that you were willing to off yourself, you could have picked a half-dozen ways that would have spared me this trouble."

Jimmy withdrew into his captain's seat, arms crossed. Nick enjoyed watching him squirm. He may regret brutalizing Jimmy in the morning, but right now it felt right. It felt like justice.

In a subdued tone, Jimmy said, "I thought if I shot myself it would be louder than the sound of the van running."

"Louder, yeah. But it would go off and stop sounding. The crazies couldn't triangulate your position with a single shot." Nick almost couldn't believe the words coming out of his mouth. He was critiquing his brother's suicide attempt, yet he continued on. "What about the baggy method. You could always have taped a big garbage bag over your head if you were too afraid of the pain. I'm assuming that's the real reason you didn't shoot yourself. You were afraid it would hurt. The only way it would hurt is if you did it like a girl and shot yourself in the chest. You weren't going to do it that way, were you? Head shots only from now on. You remember that."

Jimmy didn't respond. He gazed dully out at the road. Nick checked him a couple of times, waiting for a reply, a quip, some reaction he could counter. But like a fighter unwilling to get up, Jimmy was down for the count. Now it was time for Nick to be the grown-up again. He'd gotten whatever pleasure he could out of the situation. He'd made his brother pay for his sins a little—not enough—but as much as he was going to be able to get out of him here. Now it was time to move on. If they were going to live, to survive this nightmare, someone had to be the adult. Nick knew he was acting childishly, almost as much as Jimmy. The difference was, he told himself, he could snap out of it, get it together, and start doing what was best for both of them.

Nick continued to pace the outer city limits, tracking from one 'burb to the next. These weren't like the new subdivisions that drew you in from a main road and then dead-ended with a cul-de-sac. These were from an earlier time, a time when developers or city planners thought of these areas as just the next phase of development, which meant that the roads changed names regularly, and Nick was able to drive from one street to the next without changing his general trajectory. He didn't use a compass or even the sun that was low on the horizon. Instead, he used the city itself as his guide, his Polaris.

It wasn't strange to see the parked cars in these residential areas, but the total lack of traffic was weird. It reminded Nick of when he'd been up all night at his buddy Brian's house last summer. They'd gone out at four-thirty on a Sunday morning just to joyride. The whole town had been asleep, except for the sun itself which never sleeps this time of year. It was like they had been in on some secret and that they owned the city.

It looked that way now, and, in some ways, Nick and Jimmy were the rightful heirs of much of the city—they were the only sane ones alive in who-knows-how-many square blocks. But gone was all of that youthful triumph Nick had felt before. He didn't want the city. This wasn't his home anymore; it was its bizarro-world doppelganger with all the quaint memory inspiring twists and turns but none of the inviting resonance of a boy's home.

Nick hated to admit it, but Jimmy was right about at least one thing: they couldn't stay in Fairbanks any longer. For one, Jimmy had burned the bridge called their home. But even if they were to find another house somewhere in town, there were other reasons to leave now. Now that Nick had gotten beyond their street and had seen what was left of Fairbanks, he realized the whole city was anathema to their progress, to their future. It was too draining, too steeped in memories for them to stay and constantly be reminded of what they'd lost, what they'd never find again. No, if there was a future for them, it had to be elsewhere.

"So, we need to get some things straight," Nick said aloud. It was like his inner monologue had broken out into the audible world.

Jimmy, who had his head leaned over between the door and the passenger seat, stirred. He tilted his head, signaling he was listening but said nothing.

"Look, you don't have to talk or nothing. Just listen. I'm not sorry about what I said. You needed to hear it, a long time ago and from somebody besides me. Still, you're my brother. We're the only family either one of us has left. We're the only friends either one of us have too. We don't have to sing kumbaya or hold hands right now, but we need to at least be on the same page about a few things."

Nick saw Jimmy shift in his seat. He looked like he started to say something but stopped himself. *Good*, Nick thought, *he's got some self-control.*

"I think we should go to Deadhorse," Nick exhaled like he'd been holding his breath. He waited for a response from Jimmy, but none came. Nick continued, "I think it's kind of stupid to go, but then again, what's a better option? We can't stay here. The only friendly person we still know is up there: what's his name, Bob? And we need to get out of crazyland, which Fairbanks seems like it's going to continue to be for the foreseeable future. The Dalton Highway can get us there, and this time of year, it's passable."

Nick waited, looking at Jimmy with scrutinizing eyes. Jimmy, apparently sensing he was in the hot-seat turned and said, "You don't have to convince me. This was my idea. Let's go."

The sound of Jimmy's voice was hollow, passionless, the sound of a washed-up, emptied-out young man. It was an agreeable tone to Nick. "That's not it, Jimmy. I know you want to go. It's just…I got to be able to trust you. We have to be able to trust each other if we're going to get anywhere."

Another pause as if Jimmy was seriously considering the implications. Then he said, "I'm in."

That was all he said and all Nick could have hoped for. It was hope Nick was after anyway. The truth—whatever that was—seemed irrelevant. Nick wanted a shred of integrity, some piece of grit from Jimmy. He wanted to hear there was something or someone else inside him besides the whiny, suicidal, ruin-it-for-everyone Nancy that he knew all too well. And for now, for today, Nick had what he needed: enough to move forward.

CHAPTER 10

NICK AND JIMMY drove in silence. It wasn't the kind where they both knew what the other was thinking, the kind you have after a fight. It was peaceful, or at least Nick thought so. The sun rose higher and brighter in the sky, warming the van to the point where they would have turned on the air conditioner if the van's unit actually worked. Instead, they rolled their windows down an inch, infusing the cab with cool, morning air. They were careful—no one had to say it—to not lower the windows too much, so much that a crazy could get a hand into the van. These kinds of realities were quickly realized. The learning curve had been steep but swift.

Nick now knew where they were: no longer in the endless, rambling subdivisions but in a familiar part of town where he knew how to reach the Dalton. Jimmy must have recognized the area too, because he became alert when Nick took a turn off to the right. Jimmy's body stiffened, but he said nothing.

Nick drove slower now, more carefully because of the numerous cars strung out in the middle of what used to be busy intersections. Strangely enough, they encountered fewer crazies as they traversed the puzzle of abandoned vehicles. Nick thought it should be the other way around, but he quickly surmised an explanation: the densest parts of Fairbanks may have been like a forest fire that had already passed, burning up all the tinder. There was no fire here because it had burned so hot, so bright that it had completely consumed all its fuel. Nick hoped so. Still, reason had it that there should always be at least one crazy left, the last one standing after all the scraps.

"Hey, what are we doing?" Jimmy asked as Nick pulled into Wally's Supa-center.

"If you want to go to Deadhorse, we're going to need a few things."

Jimmy didn't argue with the rationale, but Nick could see the fear on Jimmy's face. All that talk back home about how it was easier, even safer to just go to the corner market and get more food—all that was obviously a juvenile fantasy. Now, Nick thought, Jimmy realized his foolishness at not wanting to stay and ransack abandoned nearby houses for supplies. Now, they were going into the belly of the beast.

"Look, we don't have the luxury of weighing our options. The clock started ticking as soon as you started up this van," Nick said. He saw Jimmy squirm, not wanting to go there. "I'm not starting the blame-game over again. I'm just saying we can't sit in our safe little basement and plot and plan our moves. We're on borrowed time now."

Jimmy scrunched his face. "What do you mean borrowed time?"

Jimmy's question didn't aggravate Nick; he could tell his little brother really didn't get it.

"Two things: food and fuel. We have none of one and limited amounts of the other." Jimmy seemed to realize their predicament as he slid back into his seat a bit, resigned to endure whatever Nick had decided.

Ironically, the parking lot for this mega-store was nearly empty. There was an old school bus at the far end of the lot that looked like someone had tried to turn it into their own personal mobile mansion on wheels. It was spray- painted off-white and its hubs didn't match up. Curtains were drawn, but Nick knew better than to wonder if someone was alive and unaffected inside. Even rednecks had used DataMind.

Fairbanks was a modern city, but it had its share of rednecks. You don't have to live in the South to have them. Any city where you can drive from downtown to city limits in less than an hour meant a fair share of rednecks. It was some immutable law of the universe, Nick figured, as he pulled the van close to the entrance of the store.

It felt wrong parking in front of the *No Parking—Fire Lane* sign. But those things didn't matter anymore. Nick pressed on the brake, stopping the van, but he resisted putting it into park or turning off the engine. He waited and watched. Like at home, the sound of the engine should have been enough to attract some crazies. In his inner planner, Nick had even imagined having to shoot or run over two or three before being able to enter the store. But none appeared.

Reluctantly, Nick turned off the engine.

"You ready?" Nick asked.

"No," Jimmy answered, "but that doesn't really matter."

"Two things we need to take in—flashlights," he grabbed the penlight clipped to his shirt collar, "and bang-bangs." That was Nick's poor attempt at being funny, lightening the mood a little. It was lost on his brother who dutifully checked for his light and then picked up the shotgun that was lying flat on the floor beside the center console.

Nick looked at the keys still in the ignition. He thought about leaving them; in case something happened to him, Jimmy could still get away. But in the end, he decided it was equally likely some crazy or even a desperate unaffected person might steal their ride.

"Let's go," Nick said, pocketing the keys. "Leave the doors unlocked. If things go badly, we may have to get out of here in a hurry."

Nick led Jimmy to the entrance of the store. He looked over his shoulder and watched Jimmy carry the shotgun.

"Don't muzzle me, you idiot!" Nick said more loudly than he intended.

"Don't what?"

Nick pushed the barrel of Jimmy's gun to one side. "Don't muzzle me," he repeated. "You had your barrel pointed right at me."

"I didn't have it cocked or my finger on the trigger," Jimmy said.

"That doesn't matter. One day you may forget and only *think* it isn't cocked." Nick got closer to Jimmy's face. "Can you handle this?"

Jimmy kept his eyes down at the ground. "Yeah, I'm fine."

Nick hoped so. Or, at least, he hoped Jimmy didn't shoot him in the back, accidentally, figuratively, or intentionally.

Unlike every time the boys had been in the store or the countless stores just like it, the exterior doors didn't whoosh open to greet them and there wasn't an old geezer handing out smiles and hellos at the entrance. Instead, they found the smaller side door used for emergencies. Nick pushed on it carefully, checking it to see if it was unlocked. To their surprise, the door pushed in slightly.

"Doesn't look like it was busted open," Jimmy said.

"No, and there's no broken glass anywhere. They must have just left it open."

"Why?"

Nick thought for a minute, then smiled. "Maybe the last guy whose job it was to close up went broke. Even the Wally's Supa-center chain of command was broken by the update." The smile wasn't because he could imagine someone going off their rocker but that DataMind had such a reach that even minimum-wage Wally's Supa-center employees were using it. He wondered what their perceived benefits were, what increased productivity they had experienced, and if it had really mattered in the end. Well, before the end—did it help them earn a pay raise, or were they just working at the new expected normal rate of production?

As the boys pushed their way inside, Nick wondered if the door had ever really been used. It was heavy. Maybe, he thought, I'm just weak from not eating.

The two boys maneuvered through a half-emptied rack of buggies. When they got to the front of the line where the main entrance of the store really was,

Nick told Jimmy that they both needed their own buggy.

Noisily, the two tried to separate a couple buggies that seemed like they'd been welded together. The unavoidable clanging made Nick nervous. He expected to be attacked at any second, but nothing happened. After their buggies were finally separated, the building returned to uncomfortable silence.

This part of the store was still well lit from the windows near the entrance. Nick watched anxiously for any signs of life deeper inside the store, but the shadows took over near the check-out registers. Beyond that it was pitch black. Nick listened for activity, scuffling feet, anything. Instead, he was struck by the shear silence like the curtain of darkness was some membrane through which light and sound couldn't pass. He imagined a different world on the other side.

"What should we get first?" Jimmy asked.

Nick *shooshed* him. "Be quiet."

"Why?" Jimmy said in an obligatory whisper.

"Just because no one has attacked us outside doesn't mean this whole place is empty."

"Yeah, but these buggies made so much noise. I just thought…" Jimmy trailed off.

Nick led the way, but he soon realized how difficult it was to push a buggy while holding a light and a handgun. Jimmy at least had the shoulder sling to make things easier. Finally, after a few awkward configurations, Nick resigned to place his Springfield on the little kid-seat near the handle. He told himself he would be disciplined, keeping the pistol no more than a step away.

They searched aimlessly at first, walking through the produce section and not seeing anything that excited them. Then there was the bakery and hot bar which, as they got closer, repulsed them by its putrid smell of rotten meatballs, potato salad, and other goop that even panicked unaffected people had left when they stocked up for the apocalypse. They rushed by, trying not to breathe.

As they turned a corner, Nick spoke up. "I'm thinking the outer aisle is a no-go. It's all stuff that needed refrigeration and is spoiled by now."

Jimmy nodded, but his eyes were up high where he shined his light at the aisle signs. "Look, cereal!" Before Nick could respond, Jimmy moved quickly down the aisle.

Boxes flew off the shelf as Jimmy held a hand out to one side and scooped off big armfuls of his favorite kind: Captain Kernel's Popping Puff. It was supposed to be just for little kids, and it was supposed to taste like movie-theater popcorn. Neither one was true.

"Get some Raisin-crunch too," Nick advised while he looked further down the aisle. As much as he wanted to chide Jimmy again, especially for that ridiculous brand, he knew that cereal wasn't a bad thing to stock up on. It might be mostly sugar and starch, but it would store forever, didn't need cooking, didn't need soaking, and now days they added a ton of vitamins into every box if for nothing else to ease the consciences of moms on the verge of letting their kids get the cereal they really wanted.

Further down, Nick spotted what he'd hoped to find, canned meat of all kinds. Nick decided they'd hit the jackpot with this aisle. Cereal and Spam may not sound delightful, especially to people older than them. But to two teenage boys, this was the stuff they gorged on at home when their parents weren't paying attention: calorie dense, salt ridden, preservative packed cans and boxes of awesomeness.

Nick started selecting different meats by the handful, two or three at a time. Then, as if he became conscious of their situation, he liberally scooped them into his buggy by the dozens. It would have been unadulterated fun if it wasn't for the noise. The metal cans clanged and chattered against the wire buggy like poorly tuned tines. He cringed hoping it didn't attract unwanted attention.

Nick heard Jimmy's buggy pull up behind him. Of course, Jimmy had picked the one with a squeaky wheel.

"I think we're good on cereal," Jimmy said proudly.

Nick turned and shined his light on Jimmy's buggy. It was at the point of overflowing, falling into the floor if they weren't careful.

Nick pointed his light at his own buggy. "I figure between spam and cereal—we ought to be able to live a long time."

"So, what's left?"

"I need to find a siphoning hose…"

"A what?"

"A hose to suck gas out of other cars for when we run out. Plus a gas tank. We need more batteries. Maybe oil lamps if they still have some."

"Do you think they even sell stuff like that?" Jimmy asked. "I mean, the hoses and stuff."

Their recent success finding food—two mountains of midnight snacks, actually—had rebuilt Nick's patience a little. He was only mildly irritated by his brother now.

"Yeah, they have 'em. Or they got something I can turn into one. Remember the commercial? At Wally's…"

Jimmy joined in, "if we don't have it, you don't need it."

They laughed for the first time in days.

"Alright, come on. Let's get this over with," Nick said as he wheeled his cart toward the end of the aisle.

"Let's split up. It'll take half as long," Jimmy suggested.

Nick turned and looked at his brother with suspicion. The face he saw was one of a bright-eyed, clear thinking sixteen-year-old. Not the Nancy he'd come to expect.

"You sure?" Nick wanted to trust him.

"I said I could handle it, didn't I?" Jimmy had an almost giddy expression.

"Sure. Fine. We'll meet back right here…" Nick shined his light up at the sign, "in front of check-out number six. You know where to look?"

"Yep," Jimmy answered quickly, already with his back turned squeaking away toward the aisle that had the flashlights, fire starters, charcoal, and other assorted goodies that boys sometimes went looking at when they got bored tagging along with their parents.

Nick hoped he wasn't making a mistake, but it was too late to recall Jimmy. The sooner he found what he needed, the sooner he could keep an eye on his little brother.

Nick hurried out of the grocery section of the store, past the clothing, and toward the automotive and gardening department. He knew where he was going and what he was looking for, but his mind raced as he tried to think of anything they were missing, anything he'd forgotten. This was their last real chance to stock up. He knew the road to Deadhorse wouldn't have any stores like this one.

Water, he realized in a flash. Of course, how could he be so stupid? They would need something to drink. He told himself to calm down, that it was no big deal. And it wasn't. All the check-out registers had those refrigerated cabinets with racks full of soft drinks and waters. It didn't matter they wouldn't be cold anymore. They were wet, and they'd last forever.

Toilet paper—another flash of insight. Luckily, he was close by that aisle. He took a detour and grabbed a small pack. "Ought to do until Deadhorse," he said to no one.

In the auto department, Nick spotted the red gas tanks with little trouble. He could have his pick. He could take two, three, six; it didn't matter. He decided on one. He only needed something to carry gas from one stranded car to their van. The savings in time of getting two so they could relay their efforts wasn't worth the space it took up in his buggy. He needed the extra room for sodas, he told himself.

One down, one to go, he thought as he wheeled out of the aisle. There had been no siphon hoses next to the gas cans, which was the obvious place to find them if he was going to. But he had anticipated this. He made a cursory check of the two remaining aisles in automotive, just to be sure they didn't have hoses somewhere else. Then he headed toward the gardening section.

He shined his light toward the corner of the store. As bright as the little light seemed, especially in such abject darkness, it couldn't penetrate the distance. He hoped Jimmy was lucky and had found some big beam flashlights, maybe even those that take the lantern six-volt batteries. They could come in handy, especially out on the highway.

Nick looked over toward the other end of the store where Jimmy should be. He watched the ceiling and could see a flicker of light occasionally bounce off. Jimmy was still there, he thought.

As Nick approached the gardening section, he saw what he was after. There were water hoses out in the middle aisle, apparently on sale. He examined them, not knowing what difference the price made. Most of it seemed to come down to length of hose and the material the hose was made from.

He eliminated the long hoses and compared the vinyl hoses to the more expensive rubber ones. *Which would handle the gasoline better?* It was a guess, because he had no idea. He placed the smallest vinyl hose in his buggy, but he wasn't sure. His rationale was that the gas can was plastic, so maybe the artificial hose would work better.

Just as he started to change his mind, he heard the distinct sound of glass shattering followed by Jimmy yelling his name.

CHAPTER 11

PANIC WASN'T STRONG enough a word for what Nick felt. It was worse than when from the basement he'd heard the van running in the garage. That had been the sound of potential danger. What he just heard was the sound of someone trying to kill his brother.

His legs didn't want to work, and he had to will himself to drop the garden hose. But then some sort of automatic impulse took over. He grabbed the nine-millimeter off the buggy and pulled the action back, cocking it as he ran toward Jimmy's location.

Like the time he'd made a dash to the end-zone in last year's championship game, he wasn't conscious of time or distance. He saw tunnel vision—the darkness added to the effect—until he suddenly stopped and realized he was where he expected Jimmy to be.

He shined his light frantically up and down the aisle where the lights and charcoal were. Then he heard more yelling further down toward the pharmacy.

He was close enough now that he had to keep his cool. He had to make sure he was ready to shoot but cautious enough he didn't shoot his brother by accident. He moved closer and heard the sounds of footsteps and heavy breathing.

A voice shouted, "I'm the king! Come back here."

"Jimmy, where are you?" Nick yelled.

"Over here," Jimmy said, sounding like he was in the next aisle over.

Nick jumped around the corner and shined his light to see Jimmy sprinting toward him. A large man wearing white ran ten paces behind him.

"You're not king of the mountain!" shouted the man in white.

"Shoot him," Jimmy yelled as he spun past Nick and kept on going.

Nick swallowed hard and tried not to think, not to second guess himself. This would be hard enough as it was.

Two rounds peeled off. Nick could see the man get hit, but it didn't look like he felt it. He kept coming, yelling, "Only the king gets on top!"

Nick backed up and fired. Backed up again and fired. The man was coming for him despite the obvious kinematic damage he was causing.

Nick backed into something. Realizing he had nowhere to go, he unloaded his magazine into the now staggering aggressor.

Before all his rounds were spent, Nick had the presence of mind to raise his aim. The effects from the shots to the crazy's neck and forehead were enough to spin the man sideways. He tottered, losing his balance, but still tried to run. He then fell sideways, made one final flop on the floor, and went silent, still.

Nick stood there, unsure what had just happened. A practical impulse had him pull out his second magazine from his pocket and exchange it with the empty. He racked it, and the snap made a surprisingly loud sound in the now quiet market.

Footsteps to his right. Nick shifted with his light under his pistol and spotted the source: it was Jimmy.

"Don't shoot me," he said.

Nick pointed the gun down and aimed his light back at the white and red blob in the floor. "Where'd he come from?"

"You don't want to know." Jimmy was still panting, but Nick didn't think it was from running. He sounded spasmodic, like he'd heard him when his fear got the best of him and he was holding back tears.

Nick didn't shine his light in Jimmy's face to see. He felt a bit of sympathy for his brother. His poor defenseless brother. Then it hit him: "Where's your gun?"

"Dropped it with the buggy. Over there."

Jimmy shined his light toward the pharmacy and Jimmy started walking. Nick followed.

As they passed Jimmy's buggy, Nick smelled something like the rotten soup and meatballs from the hot bar.

"What's that smell?" Nick demanded.

"You really don't want to know," was the response from Jimmy.

Soon Nick realized the source of the stench came from behind the counter somewhere.

Nick opened the door beside the counter and walked into a small hallway.

"Don't say I didn't warn you," Jimmy said behind him. As if he realized Nick was about to leave him, he moved closer and followed his older brother.

Nick turned and opened the first door on the left, the one that went behind the pharmacy counter. When he did, he almost fell down from the nauseating wave of stink that enveloped him. But he persisted in trying to open the door. It was stuck like something behind it was blocking his way.

Nick pushed, and he heard a dull thump. The door opened three-fourths of the way.

What he saw in front of him caused his jaw to drop, except the smell hit him again, forcing him to cover his mouth and nostrils with his shirt sleeve.

"I said you didn't want to know," Jimmy said. It wasn't a taunt but a sincere, regrettable tone.

Stacked systematically like the beginnings of a new Great Pyramid were more than twenty decomposing bodies. "That guy was a pharmacist?" Nick asked pointing his thumb toward the crazy he had shot. He now recognized the white lab coat he had been wearing.

Jimmy didn't answer directly. "He was the king of the mountain."

Nick couldn't tell if Jimmy was trying to be funny or what, but no one was laughing. They walked back toward Jimmy's buggy. An unstacked body slid from behind the door, helping to close it. It made Nick shudder, the heebie-jeebies all over him. He'd had enough for one day. Heck, for one lifetime.

"What were you doing over here?" Nick asked when they reached the buggy again.

"Just seeing what we might have forgotten."

"Forgotten?"

"Yeah, you know, stuff like instant coffee or paper towels." He pointed at those items in his buggy.

"That wasn't the plan," Nick said. "We were supposed to meet back at check-out six when we got done. Not go on a tour of the store. This is serious."

"I know. I thought I could handle it. I didn't think anyone else was around."

"And why didn't you shoot that crazy?" Nick looked at the Stevens single-shot. Jimmy hadn't dropped it. It was neatly placed across the top of the buggy. And Jimmy's silence was incriminating.

"I just got scared and ran," Jimmy said unconvincingly.

"No, that's not it. You didn't even have your shotgun up. What were you really doing?"

Nick's mind searched for all the possible explanations, and then it hit him.

"Empty your pockets."

"What?" Jimmy's voice rose.

"Empty them. Right now."

Jimmy had the scowl on his face, the same one he wore when Nick first shot down his idea about going to Deadhorse. But he begrudgingly emptied one pants pocket and held out its contents for Nick to inspect. Nick saw a small package of candles and slapped them out of his hands and onto the floor.

"What's that crap? I sent you to get lights, not aroma therapy, you big Nancy."

Jimmy flinched as if Nick was going to hit him.

"Aw, come on," Nick said. "Stop being a pansy and hiding from what you were really doing. Empty your other pocket."

Jimmy slowly pulled out a bottle of pills. Nick snatched them out of his hand and shined his light on them so he could read. It was labeled HYDROCODONE.

"I knew it," Nick said. "You were going to pull your junky-routine, weren't you?"

Jimmy didn't answer.

"I asked you a question. You were going to disappear on me, weren't you? Take these, get high, and check out while I drove us to Deadhorse?"

Jimmy seemed to struggle to break his silence. "Yeah, that's it."

Nick didn't like what he heard. He could always tell when Jimmy was lying. But why would he lie about this? What else could he be doing with them?

"You were going to overdose," Nick asked when it hit him.

"Probably not," Jimmy said more quickly.

Nick gave the gesture with his face and hands that said *what is that supposed to mean?* and *I give up* all at once.

"I didn't plan on taking them. Well, I was going to take them to get to sleep. But I wasn't going to overdose unless I felt like there was no alternative."

Nick stared at the bottle again. He'd heard the name of the drug before. It was fairly common, but he was trying to grasp a connection; he recognized it from somewhere.

Jimmy seemed to anticipate Nick's thought. "Mom used to take them back before DataMind. For her back. At least, at first they were for her back."

It came back to Nick in a flash. He remembered shortly after his dad and Jimmy's mom were married how she had fallen on the icy driveway outside their home that winter and had badly injured her back. He remembered seeing a similar bottle in the medicine cabinet above the sink and then later beside her bedroom table.

"*Your* mom used them. Not *mine*," Nick said impulsively.

He didn't know why it mattered, but it did. He wasn't blood kin to her. It hadn't occurred to him until now why she'd had those pills for so long, for so much time after her back seemed to have healed. She must have gotten hooked, another statistic like the ones he heard on the news. She'd seemed normal. She hadn't seemed like an addict, but now he knew she had been. Until DataMind came along. That was one of its startling claims: that there were thousands of documented cases where people had overcome substance abuse through DataMind's guided mindfulness techniques. She must have been one of the undocumented cases.

He took the bottle, squeezed it tight and chucked it as hard as he could toward the outer aisle.

"Come on. Let's get our stuff and get out of here.

DALTON

CHAPTER 12

IT DIDN'T TAKE the boys long to get their buggies out of the Wally's Supa-center. Nick continued to feel surprised by the lack of crazies surrounding the area. Their wheels squeaked loudly, and the buggies shook like miniature freight-trains. But no one came. No one seemed to hear them as they loaded up the van with their supplies.

When they finished, Jimmy said, "Watch this." He rolled his cart a few feet away and kicked it, causing it to vault over onto its side.

"Real mature," Nick said. He thought about putting away his cart somewhere. But then he realized how ridiculous his habituated thinking was. Jimmy was right. "It's the small things in life, isn't it?" he said as he ran his cart toward the parked bus nearby. It rolled fast, its wheels wobbling from the uneven pavement. Nick slammed the cart into the side of the bus. It bounced off, and he found himself doing it again and again trying to make the initial dent larger.

"Nick, there's somebody," Jimmy said.

Instantly, Nick jolted out of his juvenile destructive mode and looked back at Jimmy who was pointing to the bus. He heard a quick swish sound behind him. When Nick looked back at the bus, he didn't focus on the dented fender but up toward the side windows. An unmistakable blue-black barrel extended from one of them where the curtain inside had been drawn back.

"You care to explain why you're defacing private property?" asked a voice.

Nick instinctively threw his hands up and backed away several steps.

"Sorry, we didn't know anyone was home." He almost choked on the silliness of calling the bus a home. But this was no laughing matter.

"So, you *can* talk. Maybe you're not a crazy after all," said the man. The barrel withdrew, and the window closed.

Nick turned to Jimmy and shrugged his shoulders. He wondered if that was the end of their encounter, but then a different squeaky mechanical sound drew his attention back to the bus.

An older man, maybe in his seventies—Nick couldn't tell—descended out the side door. He held his carbine rifle to his side unthreateningly.

"I heard shooting from inside the store. You must have encountered the King." The old man wore a knit cap despite the mild summer temperatures, and his gums puckered in from not having a full set of teeth.

"Yeah, we met the King," Jimmy answered from beside the van. Nick turned and saw Jimmy walking toward them. He wanted to warn him, to tell him to stay at the van. But he knew vocalizing the idea would make the situation tenser.

"So, he's dead?" the old guy asked.

Nick didn't want to answer. He didn't trust the geezer. Not yet, anyway. But he knew his brother would talk for both of them. Jimmy was enamored by colorful people, couldn't seem to understand that they could be a threat. Couldn't understand that maybe they'd made bad choices in life the reason they lived in a bus or the reason they didn't have teeth.

"The pharmacist attacked us. I shot him dead," Nick said, surprising himself. He jumped into the conversation before Jimmy could.

"Well, I think that means I need to offer my apologies and give you thanks. See, I didn't hear you boys roll in a while ago. This is the time of day I usually sleep, and it wasn't until I heard the gunshots that I realized someone was here. I would have warned you if I'd seen you."

"It's not your fault, Mister," Jimmy said. Nick cringed at the comment. *Mister?* Jimmy sounded like a

1950s *Leave it to Beaver* rerun. Nick couldn't decide if the middle-America every-boy act was real or pretend.

"I suppose not." The old man looked off at the horizon as if his thoughts were elsewhere.

"What's the thank you for?" Jimmy insisted.

"For shooting that wacko, of course. What else?" The man had a wild look in his eye when he said *wacko*. Nick wondered if he was unstable. Then he remembered he lived in a bus. *Probably so. That or just lazy.*

"I'd like to say I was doing you a favor," Nick said, trying to keep the mood light, "but we were just defending ourselves. Same thing anybody'd do in our situation, I guess." Nicks words softened as he finished.

"It's really something, killing a man," the geezer said. This time, his expression and tone made it seem he spoke from experience.

"I'm not sure I was killing anyone," Nick said. "They were already dead the day of the update. Before then, if you think of it. They were doomed the day they tried DataMind." He wasn't sure if he was trying to convince this guy or himself.

"Already dead, huh? I've heard that one before. Boys, if I'm the first one to tell you this, I'm sorry, but we're all already dead. Born to die. We are all dead-men-walking. But only a few of us are alive. Ever."

The man gummed his mouth like he was chewing on his words. Now Nick had him pegged, he thought. He's a war-torn vet who tried to live the philosopher's life the twenty-first century way: off-grid, on the outer edge of the civilized world. That's what Alaska was: the frontier, one of the wildest places in the world, not because man hadn't been there long or hadn't tried to tame it, but because the forces of nature were so intense, brutal, and unforgiving that even if you got a leg up on the elements, they were still there reminding you that they would be waiting. That if there was a crack in the shell, in the bubble of civility, nature would rush in and take back what had been temporarily stolen from it.

"That crazy had been terrorizing this area from the first day," the man went on. "I was almost fond of him. As fond as you could be of someone who's greatest instinct was to rip you apart limb from limb and stack you on his human pyramid."

He really had seen the King, Nick thought.

"The King acted like some sort of bio-filter, it seemed to me," the man said. "He was top of the food-chain for some reason, and he seemed to clean up the place for me. Like the junkyard dog that ran off all the other strays. I didn't have to shoot as many crazies if I just gave them time to run into him; he did the killing for me. It's like police. You tolerate their violence, so you don't have to deal with the more sinister villains they bash on."

"So, I guess it's us that owe you an apology," Jimmy said, "for getting rid of the bio-filter."

Nick couldn't help but roll his eyes. This was going on too long. Clearly both Jimmy and this guy weren't the clear-thinking types. "Jimmy, we need to be going soon," Nick said. "Sir, sorry to have busted up your fender. Is there anything I can do to make it right?"

"No, you just put on some more urban camo for me. Now it looks even more abandoned. Say, where are you boys headed? I don't have to tell you how dangerous it is out here. I hope you have a nice, safe home you're staying at."

Nick shot eye-daggers at Jimmy. *We used to have a safe home*, he thought.

"We're going to Deadhorse," Jimmy answered cheerfully. He was unfazed, immune, unashamed.

"What on earth is in Deadhorse?" the man reeled.

"We've got an old family friend up there with a safe place to stay. Lots of food, fuel, generator. One of those scientific posts that are partially buried," Jimmy answered.

Nick wanted to face-palm himself. A *family friend*? They didn't know Bob. Not really.

"You should come with us," Jimmy added.

"I'm sure he's got other plans," Nick interjected awkwardly.

"Yeah, he's right, kid. Three's a crowd anyway. No, I've found my spot. You know, this is the longest I've ever parked at a Wally's without someone pecking on my window telling me to move on. I'm free now!" The man laughed at the joke that was only funny to him. "I'm going to ride it out here, boys. I've got access to food, water, everything a man really needs," he said pointing at the store. "And I'm free. I'm hiding out in plain sight where nobody can see me. I figure, all we have to do is get through one Alaskan winter. Then the wheat and the chaff will get separated automatically. Come spring, the whole world will start rebuilding, for better or worse."

The boys said their goodbyes to the man, turned, and started up their van. Nick could see in the rear-view mirror as the old man watched them from his side entrance. Then he turned and shut the fold-up door behind him.

Nick couldn't help but feel like the guy was watching over them, like they'd been his dinner guests and he was politely watching them leave his abode. Strange how civility lingered in this broken world. How, although you couldn't count on it, there was kindness from strangers. The update, he decided, hadn't made the world better, not in the aggregate. But there were aspects about this world that he appreciated.

The world going broke probably brought out both the best and worst in people.

Catastrophe was like money, sort of. They both reduced your inhibitions and compelled you to act in ways that were once unthinkable. What was the difference? Money took away your fear and made you feel bulletproof. Catastrophe rubbed your nose in despair, made the consequences of inaction or wrong action painfully obvious and swift. Somehow, they both told more about the real person than everyday life did. Everyday life made everyone the same, squished everyone into the same tiny box of conformity, of safety, of comfort. Everyday life wanted you to be an indistinguishable part of the monolithic societal whole. One in the masses. One with limited choices and just as limited outcomes. The update had changed that. For good or ill, life had become a wide-open wild card with no rules and no safety nets.

THE BOYS WERE silent for the longest time. Nick drove the old van onto the interstate bypass, something that used to be frightful for the young driver. But there, of course, was no traffic, and even if he wanted to, he couldn't get the van up to seventy miles per hour for two reasons: the van was so old and low-geared it began to shake and shimmy dangerously after reaching fifty-five, and the interstate was littered with abandoned cars which they had to carefully navigate around.

Nick expected Jimmy to chime in at any moment, questioning him about what they were doing and where they were going. But he didn't. Instead, he seemed satisfied with the moment, content to ride shotgun.

"Help me watch," Nick said as they reached a confluence of exits.

Jimmy, again, seemed to know what Nick was after. "There it is," Jimmy said after a moment. Nick saw the sign that read:

DALTON HIGHWAY - NEXT RIGHT.

Nick looked at Jimmy as if to check if he was ready, to see if he was really serious about this. Jimmy glanced over and offered his best stoic face, one that didn't look convincing at all. But it was the most Nick was going to get out of him.

Nick took the exit and almost immediately after they made the loop off the interstate, the texture and quality of the road changed dramatically. Bumps, potholes, and rough-finished pavement became the new norm. It was enough to make Nick wonder if he was making a terrible mistake. *If they don't maintain the road better than this near Fairbanks, what will it be like closer to Deadhorse?*

He drove on. The road conditions kept them moving close to thirty miles per hour, but at least it was steady. They only passed an occasional car here and there on the two-lane road. It was consistent enough that Nick felt himself relax a bit, some of the tension he'd held seemed to fade along with the sight of Fairbanks in the rear-view mirror. Nick was conscious of the sensation. He heard his body's signal loud and clear: *This is better.* But his mind wasn't convinced that the Dalton wasn't just the beginning of their troubles.

"Ground rules," Nick said suddenly.

Jimmy rolled his head back against his captain's seat and said, "Here we go." Apparently, he was feeling well enough to be snarky again.

"Do you remember what I told you back at Wally's?"

"Meet up at check-out number six?"

"No, about what we needed."

"Oh," Jimmy chuckled at himself. "Yeah, food and fuel, right?"

"So, we're good on food. More than enough to last till Deadhorse. Which, by the way, is four-hundred and three miles from here according to that sign we just passed."

"Right, which means we should arrive in . . . five and a half hours."

Nick scrunched his face and tried to figure how Jimmy came up with such an optimistic number. Then he realized. "That's assuming we're driving really fast highway/interstate speeds. To call the Dalton a highway is false advertising if I ever heard it. We're lucky to get there in twice that time. Plus, road conditions are only certain to get worse the farther north we drive."

"But there shouldn't be snow on the road this time of year," Jimmy retorted.

"I didn't say snow would block us. It's just that the roads themselves will be pitiful. I just know it. The only vehicles that go up that far are usually big trucks and they tear up the pavement real quick."

"So, what are these rules for, exactly?" Jimmy said impatiently.

"We've got to deal with the fuel problem." He saw Jimmy swing his head over to look at their fuel gauge that still read half a tank.

"Looks good to me."

"Well, fortunately you're not the only set of eyes here. Half a tank is when we should stop for refueling," Nick said.

"Don't you think that's overkill? Mom never stops until…" He stopped himself. "She never used to stop until the warning light came on."

"I remember. And it drove me nuts," Nick said. "But we're not looking at having to pull over and call someone for a lift. If we break down and there's no gas for fifty miles in either direction, what do you think's going to happen?"

"Yeah, I guess," Jimmy waived his hand, a soft dismissal. "But that still seems like unnecessary work. And aren't frequent stops more dangerous?"

Jimmy had a point there. As long as the van was rolling forward, they were safe. Jimmy couldn't get out of his sight and crazies could do little more than turn themselves into roadkill if they tried to attack them.

"You may be right." Nick hated to admit it. "But the further north we go, the fewer cars we're going to encounter. They aren't going to be plentiful like they are here, so close to Fairbanks. So, I say we make the ground rules now, ones that will work the whole way, and stick to them."

Nick could see from Jimmy's expression that his younger brother had given in. He wouldn't like it, but what else was new?

"So, how exactly do you plan on refueling anyway?"

"I'll show you," Nick said. He careened his neck as they came up on the next stranded vehicle. It was some sort of dually truck, white with a goose-neck hitch in the back. He had a bad feeling about it, but he didn't know why. He decided it could be gas or diesel, and it was better to move on.

Ahead of them loomed a shadow of a vehicle on the horizon. "Oh, man. Can you imagine what happened to that?" Jimmy asked.

Apparently, Jimmy had better eyes than Nick, which surprised the athlete. Nick didn't answer, not wanting to admit his weakness.

In a few seconds, the image became clear: a bus, a Greyhound, that had turned over on its side somehow. It blocked most of the road, only leaving enough room to get around on the margin of the left lane.

Nick could guess what had happened, but he didn't want to talk about it. Why was it Jimmy couldn't handle anything stressful or hard, but he also seemed drawn to bringing up the horror of their situation, incapable of suppressing or filtering his thoughts? Nick slowed down as they passed the blue and grey bus. Turned over like a sleeping dinosaur on its right side, it showed its underbelly to the boys. Nick figured enough of the passengers—it could have been just one—had received the update and went on a rampage. Maybe, passengers had tried to resist at first, then panic had ensued as people from the back of the bus rushed the front. Nick stopped his imagination there, just short of the scene that would have caused the driver to whip the wheel hard enough to flip the bus.

"Why don't we stop here?" Jimmy asked. "The bus ought to have plenty of fuel to get us to Deadhorse. I mean, they drive straight through all night long sometimes."

"Wrong fuel," Nick answered. "They run on diesel. Same for the big trucks we see."

Jimmy sulked a little. It didn't matter why he was wrong, or how impersonal the reason was; he always took it as a personal insult.

Less than a quarter mile up the road, Nick spotted a likely target. It was an eighties-model Chevy Nova that had more *bondo* than paint. It wasn't a common sight in this part of the country. The age and lack of collectible value meant most had been scrapped as soon as they became too expensive to repair, a long time ago. Too, most people, especially people outside the city, didn't want to drive a wimpy passenger vehicle. They usually went for a truck or SUV, something that had more horsepower and four-wheel-drive.

"Looks like our luck has changed," Nick said as he pulled over in front of the Nova.

Jimmy didn't seem to understand, scrunching his shoulders. The one thing Nick knew about Novas, or any other similar sized and aged car, was that they ran on gas. So did most of the passenger vehicles this far north. Too hard to start up a diesel in the cold when its fuel gummed up. Only the big trucks and buses that hardly ever stopped their engines utilized the more efficient fuel.

Nick looked out all the windows and mirrors before turning off his engine. They were alone. "Come on," he said as he got out of the van.

Nick reached back in for his Springfield from the middle console where'd he'd laid it. *That was it*, he realized. The thing his brain knew had been left undone when his body told him to relax.

He reached into the sliding compartment near the console where his half-empty box of nine-millimeter ammo was. He pulled out the carton of Remington UMC's and opened it carefully as if they were fragile, precious cargo. Like they would fly away if they were spooked. He counted them: twenty-three rounds. Enough to reload his empty magazine which held sixteen if you really squeezed the last one in, but not enough to replenish another mag if he should empty one.

Jimmy came around the van and watched Nick load the empty magazine. "I hope Bob has more ammo in Deadhorse," Jimmy said idly.

"I hope we don't need ammo in Deadhorse," Nick answered while trying to focus on his task. He squeezed in the sixteenth round. He had to bear down hard with his thumb to get it in. "There," he said shaking his hand for relief. He took the remaining seven rounds out of the box and placed them in his pants pocket. "Hopefully, we won't need these," he told Jimmy. "But if I do, I don't want to hunt for that box again.

The boys walked to the back of the van and opened the two rear-swinging doors. Piled on top of the spare tire and other equipment salvaged from the garage was the hose and gas tank they'd gotten at Wally's. Nick grabbed them and handed them to Jimmy.

"What do I do with these?" Jimmy asked.

Nick didn't answer but rummaged through the junk and tools that lay behind the back seat. He needed a cutting tool, but a knife seemed like too much to ask for at a time like this.

"Time to improvise," he said out loud. He grabbed Vicegrip pliers and what looked like a small chisel for woodworking. Both tools had surface rust, and he doubted either one had ever had a sharp edge on them.

He held them up for Jimmy to see, but his younger brother, clearly oblivious to the tools' functions, let alone their names, just gave a ho-hum expression. Typical Jimmy.

With Nick's detailed instructions, Jimmy pinched and gripped the hose at one end. Nick stepped on the hose and told Jimmy to pull his end up. After spending way too long miscommunicating and then trying to force a dull chisel to cut, the boys finally removed a section of hose from the metal end screw-pieces.

"There. That ought to work," Jimmy said with beads of sweat dripping down his face. The approximately six-foot length of green vinyl hose was unimpressive looking, but he held it out proudly in front of himself.

Nick walked down to the Nova that was a short distance behind the van. Jimmy shadowed him, close enough that Nick feared he would step on the back of his heel or, if he wasn't paying attention, run into him when Nick stopped. Jimmy wasn't the here-to-please type, so Nick figured it was because of what they'd been through at Wally's and before. Somehow, Jimmy had grown comfortable inside the van and must have felt exposed out in the real world. *Good*, Nick thought. *It's about time.*

Nick looked through the window into the Nova, checking for surprises. It was empty except for a bunch of fast-food wrappers on the floor of the passenger seat. "Hey, Jimmy. Dig through those wrappers. I bet there's something good at the bottom."

"No way, that looks disgusting."

"Aww, come on. You know it's just a poor man's anti-theft device."

"What is?"

"The wrappers. You could hide anything in there, leave the doors unlocked, and nobody'd ever dig through there and steal it."

For a moment, life felt normal. The kidding wasn't the mean Nancy-punishing heckling Nick had been handing out lately; it was the good-natured kind that they were both used to, that they both enjoyed even.

Jimmy, he had noticed, still had his phone. Nick could see its imprint on his rear pants pocket. Jimmy must have brought it with him when he had tried to take a dirt nap in the garage. Nick could have asked him what time it was, but he didn't. Instead, he raised his eyes to the sky. The sun was hiding behind clouds, but it appeared to be midday. That's all that he needed to know.

Nick started to open the Nova driver's side door but thought better of it. On a car this old, he doubted it had a gas tank release button. Sure enough, the door to the tank opened easily making a squeak. Beneath it was the exposed port with the screw-cap missing. Nick figured it had probably been lost for decades.

"Now what?" Jimmy asked. "How do you get the gas to come out?"

Nick's faced scrunched up again in disbelief at his younger brother's lack of know-how. "It's called a siphon. Didn't you ever see dad get the old gas out of the boat's tank?"

"No," Jimmy answered quietly. Nick started to argue with him, to try to remind him of the instances. But then he remembered the timeline. Nick's dad hadn't had a boat since before he had married Jimmy's mom. That memory was Nick's alone. In fact, he was the only one in the entire world who probably still remembered that old fiberglass jon boat.

"Open the gas can lid and put it on the ground here," Nick directed. Nick stuck one end of the hose down into the car's tank. It was a tight squeeze, but it was going. He pushed until it met resistance and was ostensibly at the bottom of the tank. Grabbing the other end of the hose, Nick took a deep breath as if he were about to jump into the deep end of a pool. He sucked hard on the hose and was surprised by the amount of force he had to apply. He wasn't even sure he was making progress. He had intended to put his thumb on the hose in between sucks, but he was too afraid he'd lose pressure to do that. Instead, he maintained the seal with his mouth and took breaths through his nose.

Then he felt the temperature change in the middle section of hose he held with his left hand. He pulled the hose out of his mouth quickly and smashed his thumb over-top the end. Then he jammed the hose down into the empty can. The gas trickled into the five-gallon can, and both boys breathed a sigh of relief. For Jimmy, it was probably just because it had worked at all, but Nick was glad he hadn't swallowed gasoline. It could kill you or, at least, give you a really bad day.

The boys watched reverently as the gas, as much a symbol of life as food was, slowly filled the can. "When this nears the top, I want you to hold the hose the way I did. Keep the gas from running out on the ground."

Jimmy nodded his head in agreement. *Surely, he can handle that*, Nick told himself. "Okay, now," Nick said before the gas reached the top. Jimmy pulled out the hose and clamped his thumb down stopping the flow. He had a short grin, a look of self-pride.

Nick screwed the lid on top of the can and took it back to the van. Something he hadn't allowed for was the difficulty in pouring the now forty-pound gas can. And he really needed a funnel to reach the gas port perfectly. But he didn't have time or resources for perfection. He had to make it work.

Awkwardly, Nick smashed the can between the van and his body to help support the weight as the gas trickled into the van more slowly than Grandpa Joe used to pee when his prostate was giving him trouble. Nick smiled at the memory and looked over at Jimmy who took the smile as if it was directed at him. He returned it, but Nick withdrew his.

After Nick finished pouring—it all almost poured out—he took the empty-ish can back to the Nova.

"Let me do this one," Jimmy said.

"No arguing from me," Nick said, although he actually had his doubts that his brother could do anything right. Nick dropped the can down in front of Jimmy.

"Um. Could you get the lid off? I only have one hand free."

Nick exhaled, showing his frustration. He wanted to say, *I thought you wanted to do it*, but he didn't want to start something.

Nick opened the can and walked back to the van. As he walked he heard the trickle of gas starting to flow into the can. Good, he thought. He wasn't sure how much gas the Nova had, and he didn't know how large the van's tank was. He figured the van had a large one, maybe twenty gallons or more. So, two cans might equal half a tank. That was the estimate.

He walked to the van's still open driver's side door and pulled the hood release. Then he went around and found the final release in the front grill. His eyes were on the Dodge Ram hood emblem, an iconic ram, when the hood popped up higher. He imagined the silver ram bashing its way through cars and crazies, clearing a path for them.

He raised the hood and pretended to inspect the engine. He knew a little, like where to pull the oil dipstick; it was half a quart low and black as tar. It may have been years since it had been changed. Brake fluid looked okay, and so did the power steering. His dad, before DataMind, had shown him a little about car maintenance. He couldn't check the radiator for coolant. It was too hot, but the overflow reservoir had some bright green liquid—a good sign, he figured. The only thing left that he knew to do was check the automatic transmission fluid, but the engine had to be running to do that.

He walked back to the driver's seat and turned on the ignition. The van squealed one of its belts briefly, then roared back to life.

"What are you doing?" Jimmy yelled.

"Gotta check something. Don't worry about it."

Nick *was* checking something, but he knew it mattered little what the results were. At least, he couldn't do much about it if there was a serious problem, not unless he was lucky and there was an extra quart of fluid in the van somewhere. At this point, checking was just to eliminate the unknown, and only for the time being. Everything was temporary. But if he knew his fluids were topped off, he could stop worrying they were going to suddenly break down.

The red transmission fluid dripped from the stick, and Nick happily put it back and closed the hood. He turned his back on the van and looked at the mountains in the distance. He thought about turning off the engine, but he liked this moment and wanted to be still for a minute. Away from Jimmy. Away from problems.

"Nick! Nick!" yelled his brother.

Nick turned and saw Jimmy come running.

"We've got to go. Come on," Jimmy said, grabbing his arm.

"What is it?" Nick asked. But before Jimmy could answer, Nick spotted trouble south on the Dalton.

CHAPTER 13

NICK DIDN'T WANT to move. He'd had too many of these experiences already today. There was a lag between his mind and body, but finally his legs started moving with or without the rest of him.

"Let's go. Let's go," Jimmy begged as they climbed into the van, Jimmy first, through the driver's side door, then Nick.

Nick looked in the rear-view mirror. The back doors were still open, and in the distance, he could see a faint figure growing steadily larger. Someone was running towards them.

"Let's go," Jimmy chanted.

"Where's the can and hose?" Nick asked.

"We don't have time for this. Come on. Let's get moving."

"Jimmy," Nick said turning to him, "where's the tank and hose?"

"Outside, by the Nova. I left them."

Nick jumped out of the car.

"Where are you going?" Jimmy shrieked.

"Get in the driver's seat. Keep the engine running. Be ready to drive when I tell you."

Nick didn't wait for a reply or to see Jimmy crawl behind the wheel. If Jimmy's sense of self-preservation wasn't strong enough to do this, then…

Nick knew they needed the can and hose because they would run out of fuel again, long before Deadhorse. And without these items, they would be up the creek with no way to siphon gas.

He sprinted toward the Nova, but when he spotted the running man, part of his insides twisted like he was going to throw-up. His body obviously didn't want to run toward danger. Even his legs turned numb and shook from the adrenaline.

The crazy was within fifty yards, half a football field, away when Nick reached the tank and hose. Jimmy had left the hose loose on the ground; gas was trickling out onto the pavement, and Nick had to yank the hose out of the Nova quickly. More gas flung onto his shoes and splattered on his face and torso. He tucked the hose awkwardly under one arm and bent down for the can.

There wasn't time to turn and face his assailant, though he could now hear his footsteps and the wheezy drone of madness coming toward him. Nick ran for the van as fast as his sloshing and banging gas can would let him.

He didn't have much time to think or plan. He simply jumped into the back and yelled for Jimmy to drive.

The engine whined high and loud but there was no movement.

Nick climbed over the back seat just as the crazy reached the back of the van.

He turned and was met by the slobbering face of a long-haired man who tried to grab him. Nick reeled backwards. It was like every bad dream he'd had about stepping into a pit of vipers with nowhere to escape.

The crazy didn't miss a beat but continued trying to climb over the seats after Nick. The engine whined high, but the van wasn't moving.

"Get it out of park and into drive!" Nick yelled as he pulled out his Springfield.

There was a short lull in the engine roar. Then the old van lunged forward and one wheel tried to squeal.

Nick fell backwards from the momentum shift, but the crazy seemed to recover easily and grabbed Nick's shirt with both hands. He pulled Nick tight like he was trying to rip off his clothes. Nick had his gun in his right hand, but he was wedged so tightly against the back seat he couldn't raise it.

"Jimmy!" Nick needed help, but he didn't know what or how.

Nick smelled the foul stench of the crazy's breath as he wheezed from the who-knows-how-far run.

The crazy's grip tightened more and Nick realized he wasn't trying to rip his clothes off; he was trying to tear the flesh off his bones. The fingers felt like ice picks squeezing harder and harder into his shoulders where the man had him.

"What do you want me to do?" Jimmy yelled.

Now it was Nick's turn to sound like a crazy. The blinding pain produced a howl from him that he didn't recognize; it wasn't his voice.

Consciousness felt slippery, like the pain was throttling up and down and when it was up the sound of his own pain drowned out his thinking. In one of the dips, Nick had a thought: "Brake hard!"

Jimmy stomped the brake, and Nick was torn out of the crazy's grip like ripping off the mother of all band-aids.

There was a clang as Nick's pistol fell out of his hand and ricocheted off the back of the driver's seat and onto the floor. Nick saw the gun and the eyes of the crazy who seemed to realize the threat. Nick—his arms didn't want to work—scuffled over to the handgun, racked it as the crazy was halfway over the back seat, turned and shot the man three times.

The sound of the explosive gas escaping from the four-and-a-half-inch barrel was loud enough to make your ears ring when you shot outdoors. Inside the van, the shots made it feel like it was you getting shot, the sonic blasts threatening to tear out your insides.

The crazy fell backwards and out of the van, not from a point of retreat but from the precarious unbalanced position he had been in when Nick shot him.

"Go, Jimmy," Nick commanded.

The van started moving. As Nick stood to look over the back seat, he saw the crazy on his feet again. He was badly wounded; blood gushed from his torso, from obviously fatal wounds.

Nick locked eyes with the man, trying to see if he realized his fate. Nick hated the thing's guts, but he still had the instinct to empathize with another human being, especially one that was dying.

But the eyes Nick saw didn't look human. They were white and brown alright, but there was no transfer of communication, no sense of consciousness, no display that the man saw Nick as another person, no recognition. No one was home. At best, the man wasn't a man at all. Just a wild animal hell-bent on killing them.

Despite fatal wounds that would soon cause him to go unconscious, the crazy showed no concern for itself but continued trying to run after the van.

Nick raised his pistol, lining up the man's head with its sights. He slowly pulled the trigger and another overwhelming sonic blast echoed through the van. It was enough for Jimmy to flinch, twisting and swerving the wheel momentarily before adjusting.

Nick bounced to one side, then pulled himself upright. When he looked out the back, the creature that was once a man lay still on the pavement.

"What was that for?" Jimmy asked.

Nick didn't answer, but he had his reasons. And it wasn't because the man was trying to chase them again. There was no chance he would have caught up to them while the van was running. Plus, at any second he was about to bleed out. No, Nick shot him to finish the job. To put to rest that tiny doubt that this crazy was still out there when Nick would try to sleep tonight. To eliminate the risk that there had been some small part of that man that was still human, some scrap of humanity trapped inside forced to watch helplessly as the monster controlled its actions. Nick remembered that Bible verse Grandpa Joe used to quote. Something about how the end of things was better than the beginning.

CHAPTER 14

AFTER A FEW miles, the boys stopped the van. Nick wanted to make sure they hadn't lost the gas can and hose. Fortunately—somehow—the crazy hadn't kicked them out the back during the scuffle. Nick emptied what was left from the can into the van's tank. Then he returned the can to the back and closed the doors.

The smell of gas was strong. It was on his shirt and, especially, his shoes. He wondered how long it would take for the fumes to dissipate. Now, gasoline no longer seemed like a symbol of life; their recent close encounter had forever tainted that imagery.

After they got going again, Nick took mental stock of their situation. Jimmy was riding shotgun, so far unscathed minus a few close calls and a failed attempt to kill himself. *Not bad for the apocalypse*, Nick snickered to himself.

The van had been running surprisingly well. It was old. The odometer said it had ninety-eight thousand miles on it. Nick could only hope those were the original miles. He remembered his dad explaining how old cars weren't built to last like new ones and that way back there they didn't even bother making odometers that went past one-hundred thousand. Nick hoped the van had never rolled over to zero before.

And how was Nick? he asked himself. There was no reply, no voice inside that answered. He was alive, he figured. And that's all you could ask for right now. And they had plenty of food. The gas they'd gotten from the Nova almost filled up the van's tank which was good enough for a few hours, at least.

Outside, the terrain was rough but stable. They were driving on asphalt but not the kind that they usually made interstates and major highways out of. To Nick it looked more like the kind of rough, black tar-infused stuff they had poured for the outdoor basketball court at his middle school years ago. That stuff stunk the whole time he was a student there. He bet it still smelled. And they wonder why kids are getting cancer, he told himself.

The one disconcerting thing—although Nick had anticipated it—was that there were now fewer cars on the road. It made driving easier, but securing more fuel would be problematic. Now more than before, Nick felt that his rule about stopping at a half-tank was the right choice.

A new exterior feature emerged. It had become a welcomed sight, almost like an adopted pet, a wild animal that comes to visit your bird feeder or eat from your vegetable garden. You can't really touch it or pet it, but you name it and you like to see it come around. The gas and oil pipeline ran parallel to the Dalton on the east side of the road. It wasn't that impressive on the face of it. There were surely shinier and larger structures in Fairbanks, but out here in the wilderness it was a touch of civilization and it was a constant. It ran—so Nick had been told—all the way to Deadhorse and the end of the Dalton Highway.

Nick, the constant planner, imagined what they'd do if the van broke down. Naturally, he told himself, they'd walk. But he didn't see Jimmy and himself trekking down the highway. There would be too many crazies like the one they had met at the Nova. Instead, he saw himself walking beneath the belly of the pipeline on top of the fresh summer grasses that caribou were apt to eat.

That was a pretty fantasy, Nick realized, and he snapped out of it. He didn't want to let himself escape. Not yet. Not until he knew they were out of danger. That was the risk of planning too much, being so inside your head you didn't know what was really going on around you.

He brought his attention back to the stranded cars. Two thoughts: would there be enough vehicles with gas to get them to Deadhorse? He thought so, but there wasn't any way to know, really. Second, he wondered how the drivers of these cars had all come to be there. Why had they parked where they did? The Greyhound they'd seen made sense; some guy had been using the DataMind update on the bus and went broke. But what about all the drivers of passenger vehicles? As far as Nick understood, the DataMind app required users to plug in earbuds and focus their attention on the screen of their devices. He'd seen his dad and stepmom use it before, and they'd even warned him not to look at the screen, fearing it would affect him somehow. There's no way this many cars and drivers were out here getting the update, he thought. They couldn't drive and meditate at the same time, no matter how good at multi-tasking the app had made some people. The only solution was that the update had some kind of delayed effect, which explained why there had been an outpouring of initial complaints the same day everyone went broke. People must have used the app, noticed it didn't make them feel right. But by then, it was too late. The drivers on the Dalton must have used the app that morning, gotten in their cars to go to work in the next town over, and went broke on the highway.

Nick spotted the sun on his left in the western sky. He knew it wouldn't set today, but he could tell by its relative position it was late afternoon. He looked at

Jimmy. He was jamming out on his phone. He felt like criticizing him for using up the battery further, but then he noticed a twelve-volt adapter plugged into the cigarette lighter. Nick was glad to see it was there, but he was flustered by it at the same time. How was it Jimmy had had the presence of mind to bring his phone and a charger but he couldn't think through the problem of starting the van in the garage and attracting every crazy in a square mile? And who brings a phone charger to their suicide party? Only people who don't think they're really going to die, that's who.

Nick fumed and fretted but kept it all inside. Someone had to be the adult. He knew if he pushed Jimmy, it would just make things worse. Miserably worse. He could hold it in until he got to Deadhorse, he told himself.

But what he couldn't do was drive the rest of the way. The last road sign said it was two-hundred ninety-five miles away, and Nick's eyelids were getting heavy.

He checked the fuel gauge one more time. It was still at three-quarters of a tank.

"You feel like driving?" Nick asked.

Jimmy pulled his earbuds out and said, "Huh?"

"I'm getting groggy. You feel like driving?"

Jimmy was slow in answering. "Yeah, sure." It wasn't the sound of someone ready to assist. Nick held in his criticism. He knew that if sparks flew, Jimmy might refuse to drive entirely.

Nick pulled over and climbed into the back seat.

"Just keep it around thirty-five," Nick instructed as Jimmy crossed over the console into the driver's seat. "That seems to be the sweet spot." Nick expected Jimmy to complain about how it was too slow or how he didn't need someone to tell him to drive, but he didn't. If anything, he seemed grateful for Nick's instructions.

"You gotta dodge two things," Nick continued. "Cars and potholes. And you have to stay on the highway, which shouldn't be hard to do. Most of the side roads aren't fully paved, so you'll know if you screw up." Again, Nick felt like he was assuring himself more than Jimmy, but Jimmy received it earnestly.

"What are you doing?" Jimmy asked.

It took a second for Nick to understand. "If I can, I'll be sleeping back here."

Jimmy nodded passively.

"Oh, I almost forgot," Nick added. "You've got to stop when the gauge reads half-empty."

"Don't you mean half-full?"

Again, confusion. The dumb grin on his younger brother told Nick he was trying to make a joke. "Yeah, whatever. Just don't forget."

Nick sat down Indian-style on the open space between the front and back seats. There were metal cleats where a second row of seats used to be. He tried to look for something that would substitute for a pillow, but all they had were guns, cereal boxes, and spam cans. Finally, he curled up in a ball, extended his right arm outward, and rested his head on it poor-man style. He knew he was apt to get a crook in his neck that way, but what was his alternative?

He tried to relax, feeling the driveshaft underneath the car rumble and spin as Jimmy accelerated. But there was something in the way, something itching that he couldn't scratch, and the sandman refused to scratch it for him. Then it occurred to him: *Jimmy doesn't know how to drive.* Well, he had a learner's permit. But he'd kept it despite turning sixteen back in March. Their parents had been bugging him about getting his license, but he had kept making excuses. Nick hadn't wasted time thinking about it before, except what it took to tease Jimmy.

Nick wondered if Jimmy had put off testing for his license because he had been scared of driving or because he had enjoyed the VIP treatment of being carted around. Nick had given him a hard time, but he had still dutifully driven him to high school and back home every day. It hadn't bothered Nick much, because Jimmy had never asked to be taken anywhere else. Well, almost never. Except for the card and game shop downtown, the nerd headquarters of the world, Nick had called it.

It was a heck of a time to learn, Nick decided, but learn Jimmy must. Their very lives depended on it now. No matter how cozy this place in Deadhorse was or wasn't, Jimmy would have to grow up and know how to do things for himself. Despite the epic uncertainty it created in the world, the update had made a few things clear as crystal: no one was coming to save you. Second chances weren't guaranteed. And you were responsible for your own life, your own well-being. If you came up lacking, you'd get through your short list of people to blame so fast your head would spin. And you'd know—you'd have to know—mistakes were yours alone. Sharing blame was like sharing food, gas, shelter; no one had to do it anymore. If you shared anything with anybody, it was by choice. You knew it, and they knew it. It was simple that way.

Nick released his esoteric ruminations, and the inner wheel of pictures, sounds and senses spun wildly, allowing him to drift away into sleep.

CHAPTER 15

NICK AWOKE TO the sound of Jimmy running over the world's biggest wake-up strip, or so he thought. His mostly still asleep mind had him grabbing for the wheel that he believed Jimmy had relinquished. But Nick was still on the floor of the van, and when his eyes saw clearly, he could see Jimmy still steering with hands on ten-and-two.

"What's happening?" Nick snapped.

"The road's really rough for some reason," Jimmy said.

Nick stood up, his legs a little wobbly, and the crook was in his neck as he'd expected. He moved forward to look at the road in front of the van. He could tell some time had passed—he couldn't tell how long—by the change in the sun and the more subdued color of early evening.

Despite the dimmer light, Nick could see pretty well. And the road looked fine. As fine as the Dalton could look, anyway.

"No, something's wrong. Pull over," Nick commanded.

Before the van had come to a full stop, Nick slid open the heavy side door and jumped out. He nearly twisted an ankle in his haste as the road beneath him refused to move with his body's inertia. He recovered and double checked his Springfield tucked under his belt behind him.

Then he made a quick visual assessment of their surroundings: no cars, no crazies, no problems.

Except there *was* a problem. A big one that wasn't just going to go away.

"How'd you do this?" Nick almost screamed.

Jimmy came around the back of the van and saw the completely flat tire on the back passenger side wheel.

"Oh, man," Jimmy said.

"What did you run over?"

"I didn't see or feel anything in the road. Nothing unusual. It just started feeling funny. Nick, I didn't know it was flat."

Nick waived him off, not wanting to hear more excuses. "It's good I heard it when I did," Nick said. "You can't just keep driving on a flat tire. The wheel will warp. Then you're really screwed."

Nick said it like he knew what he was talking about. But he was just repeating what his dad had told him a long time ago. How would he even know if the wheel was warped? He couldn't tell just by looking at it.

Jimmy followed Nick back to the rear of the van as he opened the two doors. Some of the spam cans spilled out onto the road.

"Pick those up, would you?" Nick told more than asked. Jimmy began picking up the cans. Then Nick spilled more cans and cereal boxes out as he grabbed the full-size spare tire out of the back. It was heavier than he thought it would be. He dropped it down onto the road, and it bounced. That was a good sign, he figured. No use having a spare tire if it wasn't full of air.

He rolled the tire around the door and set it next to the flat tire. He looked at the flat again. He thought flat tires hissed, but this one was so long gone that it didn't look like there was a single breath of air in it. In fact, he saw the metal belts working their way through the tire where the tread had started to tear away against the grind. He'd heard about the belts, the impossible sounding metal belts inside tires, but he'd never seen one before. *Lucky me*, he thought.

"Jimmy, can you bring me the jack?"

Jimmy didn't answer, but Nick could tell he was looking for it by the sound of stuff being moved around in the back of the van.

Then, hesitantly, Jimmy said, "I can't find it."

Nick started to describe it, but instead he got up and stomped his way to the back of the van. "If you want something done right…" he said under his breath.

Nick stared into the back of the van. He saw Jimmy holding a tire wrench. "Where is it?" Nick asked.

"That's what I'm saying. I don't see it."

"No, where did you put it?"

"I don't . . ."

"You've got to be kidding me," Nick exhaled. This was all they needed. "Why would you bring the tire without a jack? I thought I told you . . ."

Nick stomped back around to the flat tire, squatted down, and stared at it pointlessly.

Jimmy scuffled back around. "Nick, I don't even know what a jack looks like, let alone what you do with one."

"Don't play stupid."

"I'm not. I didn't know."

Jimmy probably was telling the truth, but the truth didn't matter right now. Not the kind that told you the difference between guilty, innocent, responsible for, or culpable. Distinctions without a difference now.

"We're screwed, and it's your fault, Nancy."

"It's not my fault the tire blew out."

"Oh yeah? Who was driving?"

Jimmy winced and scrunched up his face. He was going to that place again, but Nick didn't care. "When is it ever your fault, Jimmy? I mean, when do you ever stand up and take responsibility for your mistakes?"

"These are old tires on an old car driving on a rough road. It could have happened to you just as easily," Jimmy insisted.

"Yeah, but we'd still be without a jack for the spare tire. And whose fault would that be? Yours—that's who. If I'd grabbed the tire, I would have grabbed the jack lying next to it. I know I told you to do it, which is bad enough. I have to tell you things like get the tire *and* the jack. I have to say things like don't get us both killed. I have to say things like don't make a bunch of noise and attract crazies, or don't be a junky, or quit being a sissy momma's boy all the time."

Jimmy dropped the tire wrench which banged loudly on the pavement, then walked a few steps away to the front of the van and stared off defiantly into the distance. Nick stared at the problem, the perfectly good tire with no tools to get it on.

Nick was too mad for his brain to work right. He didn't see a way forward. It seemed impossible. All he could think of was all the ways they couldn't: couldn't replace the tire, couldn't carry all their food with no bags, couldn't walk the rest of the way to Deadhorse, couldn't go back to Fairbanks, couldn't survive out here when winter came. It was the ultimate impasse.

"Nick," Jimmy said quietly.

"I'm not in the mood for more excuses," Nick said, not looking at his little brother.

"Nick, look," he said louder.

Nick stood and turned to see Jimmy pointing toward the pipeline. In the distance, maybe two-hundred yards away, were more than a dozen dark figures lined up underneath the pipeline. They were people or, at least, were human shaped. They stood at arms distance from each other.

Neither boy said anything. Then a change. Something under the pipeline moved. Three images. Three shadows lunged toward them, running fast. Faster than a man could run.

"Dogs!" Jimmy yelled.

"Get in the van," Nick commanded. He racked his Springfield and looked back toward the pipeline. The impossible situation worsened as the row of figures started moving toward them, following after the vanguard line of dogs.

CHAPTER 16

NICK SLAMMED THE sliding van door loudly as if it mattered how hard he did it, like the approaching danger could be kept out only if he tried hard enough.

"Get the shotgun," Nick ordered.

"We can't take them all on," Jimmy said as he grabbed the Stevens single-shot.

Nick didn't answer but thought about it. *Did they have enough ammo for that many crazies?* He knew he had two magazines, thirty plus shots. That meant he roughly had two shots for each of them. Plus a couple extra in his pocket.

Jimmy had—what use was what Jimmy had? He was as likely to accidently shoot his brother instead of helping. Still there a shotgun, and it had five shells on the wrap on the stock and what looked like a dozen more on the sling bandolier.

"Maybe," he said out loud. *Maybe we can hold them off if we're fierce enough.*

"We're going to funnel them," he told Jimmy. "They may break a window when they get up here. We can't stop that. But we're going to give them one option and hope they use it. That way we can fill their faces with gunfire when they attack."

Nick wasn't sure he was doing the right thing as he rolled down the passenger side window, the one facing the attackers. But there was no time to think.

Nick looked out at the pipeline. The figures were gone, but he knew they were down in the little valley hidden between them and the pipeline. The dogs yelped as they rounded the top of the hill.

Jimmy watched from the back seat as Nick raised the Springfield toward the dogs. There was no way he was going to hit these moving targets, he knew. But he fired twice anyway, ripping up the dirt near them.

The barks of the dogs changed, became whinier, sensing danger.

Then there was a high-pitched whistle, and the dogs stopped, turned, and ran the other way.

Nick and Jimmy exchanged glances. A good break, maybe.

Nick maintained his aim toward the east as the figures began to crest the hillside. No longer dark shadows, Nick saw several men's faces, some with long dark hair, all with dark complexions.

"They're natives!" Jimmy said triumphantly.

Nick swallowed hard, holding back the hopeful emotion that had sprung up at the realization. "Natives can go broke too," he said.

But he was hoping just like Jimmy that these were unaffected people.

He pulled back his Springfield, not wanting to appear more aggressive than was necessary. But he held it with both hands below the window just in case.

When the dozen or so men topped the hill, they stopped. They were about thirty yards away, Nick figured. About as far as he could reasonably throw a football and expect to hit his target.

A man that looked much like the others stepped forward from the line. "Hello!" he yelled.

He neither sounded friendly or aggressive. A neutral posture, which was what Nick would assume. Nick yelled hello back.

Then there was nothing. No words. No movement. Just a stare-down.

After reaching some sort of mental boiling point, Nick grabbed the handle to the passenger-side door and opened it. The click it made plus the squeak of the oil-thirsty door ruined the silence.

"What are you doing?" Jimmy asked.

"What I have to." Nick had expected Jimmy to be the one to break ranks, to trust a stranger. He always had been. But for a reason he couldn't explain, Nick stepped out of the van and put his Springfield on the ground. He raised his hands in a gesture that didn't signal surrender but peace.

Nick heard the sliding door to the van open. It was Jimmy coming out. He did the same thing with the shotgun.

Slowly, the man who had spoken before walked toward them. He maintained eye contact with Nick as if he was testing him, looking for some sign to distrust them.

When he reached the side of the road, the man stopped. "Thought you were crazies," he said in a calm voice. "That's why we sent the dogs. Crazies hate dogs for some reason."

"I wasn't too happy to see them either," Nick said.

"How'd you know we weren't crazies?" Jimmy asked.

"You got in the van. A crazy would have just started running. They don't reason, they just act out of emotion. Pure emotion."

There was another lull, a moment when the native man examined the boys, eyeing them over. Finally, Nick stepped forward with his hand out. "My name is Nick."

The man didn't step forward to meet him but did extend his hand. He held a scoped hunting rifle between his arms. "I'm Pete," he said. They shook hands. Nick smiled, but Pete maintained his solemn expression.

"This is my younger brother Jimmy."

"Just a year-and-a-half younger," Jimmy said as he shook Pete's hand.

"It's not safe for you two to be up here by yourselves," Pete said. He spoke from some secret script like there was an inner dialogue that only occasionally surfaced. Nick wondered if this was because he was being cautious or whether this was just his way.

"You're telling me," Nick finally answered. The timing was off, and it didn't sound as funny as Nick meant it to be.

Pete looked over at the flat tire. "I see you had some car trouble."

"Yeah, I don't guess you have a jack handy?" Nick asked.

"No." The man paused. "Tell me, where are you headed." He looked up and down the highway. "This is no place for two young boys to be. Not before the world went broke. Especially not after."

Nick was surprised the natives used the same lingo about the update. He figured they heard some of the same reports on the radio or TV before they went off the air. These groups practiced a strange mix and match of traditional ways and modern western lifestyle. Or that's what his parents had always told him. Besides school field trips when he was in third grade, he hadn't really interacted with many Native Americans. And in third grade, he remembered the reservation being a total tourist trap; all the people dressed up in evocative garb that probably wasn't even authentic to this part of the continent. Everybody had to make a buck some way.

"We know someone in Deadhorse," Nick said. "He invited us to stay with him before we lost power and communications in Fairbanks. Then we had a flat and…" He paused, choosing his words wisely. "*We* forgot to bring a jack. So now *we're* stranded."

Pete seemed to relax a bit as if he'd heard enough details to believe their story. "Deadhorse is a long ways from here. Too far to travel by foot." He looked up and down the road again. "And it's not safe to stay here."

Nick didn't know what to say. He wanted to be sarcastic: *You think? Well, gosh. I'd never thought of that.* But he bit his tongue. It seemed more likely that Pete was trying to talk himself into something than convince the boys.

Pete looked at the ground. Then he looked up. "You should come with us to our village."

Nick responded, "I'm not sure—"

"Yes," Jimmy interrupted. "We'd be glad to. Thank you."

There was the Jimmy Nick knew.

161

"You'll be safe with us. And in the morning, we can bring tools back here and help you get on the road again."

Pete looked to Nick, seeming to know that it was Nick who made the real decisions.

"Are you sure?" Nick asked.

Pete nodded yes.

"Well, we'd really appreciate the help.

"Come on," Pete said, turning to walk toward the pipeline. "We need to move if we're going to get home by supper time." Nick caught part of a smile on Pete's face, the first one he'd seen.

CHAPTER 17

THE WALK BACK to Pete's village had lasted more than an hour, but Nick felt like they'd walked for days and that they were no longer in the same time and place they had been back at the Dalton. Instead, they'd been transported back in time to a world that was simpler, one in which man and nature had a working agreement that was tested daily. Nick couldn't keep his romantic notions about the natives from kicking in. It was such a strong impulse that he was repeatedly alarmed when he would look at one of the men and realize they were wearing blue jeans, a store-bought coat, or some other modern item of clothing that didn't fit his conception of how they should dress.

The natives may not have perfectly resembled their ancient ancestors, but their surroundings looked the same as they had for thousands of years. Nick was sure of it. Once they'd passed the pipeline—what a mammoth structure that was when you got right up to it—all semblance of civilization seemed to disappear, replaced by crystal clear creeks, knee-tall meadows, and mostly coniferous forests.

The men had been nearly silent when they started their trek. Nick couldn't help but feel a bit out of sorts, and the fact that the men let them walk right in the middle of their line made him feel almost like a prisoner. Or maybe a captured animal. They were the savages; Nick and Jimmy were their captives. Gosh, why did his mind go to such stereotypes, such cartoonish imagery? He couldn't help it, he told himself. He wasn't racist or prejudiced. Not really. It was just all those stupid movies he'd seen as a kid. As long as no one tried to tie them up and carry them on sticks over their shoulders, he'd be fine.

The party started climbing elevation, and the terrain became a patchwork of birch and pine. The men chatted in their native tongue, and Nick wondered if that meant they were close to home. The sound of the words had that wispy, soft quality he'd heard before, a generic impression of all Native American tongues. He remembered learning in school how people had migrated over the Bering Strait more than ten thousand years ago from Asia. He wondered what was really true, if anyone could really prove that, or if it was just a fashionable thought. Propaganda even.

The world of yesterday seemed like a lie. It was never coming back, he realized. So why trust anything he'd been told there? Why assume that version of reality/civilization/life had anything honest to say? It and most of its denizens had all gone broke, hadn't they? What evidence was there that he could trust anything he'd ever thought was true? None, he told himself. If anything, there was evidence to the contrary. Life, God, the Universe—something had judged his world, the old world. He was a transient, a survivor, a relic. If he made it into the next age, he would have to become good at decoupling from the world he remembered. Nick told himself this was true. This was the truth now. Survival meant forgetting.

The men's voices grew louder and noticeably happier as the first hint of smoke was detected by Nick's nose. Soon the forest seemed to change. There were tree stumps here and there, and the forest floor seemed to be clear of brush and debris. This was human habitation, Nick realized. The world around him was still a natural system, totally biological, but the conditions had been altered, tweaked by the human creatures that inhabited the environ.

The mountain slope leveled off a bit and they came to a small mountain stream that ran perpendicular to their path. But the men and the path turned left and followed a new trail, one that followed the little brook. Nick paid more attention to the terrain that lay before them. The trees became increasingly sparse, and soon they were in some sort of partial clearing or bald. The smoke that he'd only smelled before was now visible, rising above the remaining tree line.

Pops and cracks echoed through the quiet woods. Then Nick saw two young boys running toward them. His first instinct was to grab his Springfield, but then he realized he'd left his gun back at the van. It had seemed like the thing to do.

The youngsters pulled up to the caravan with animated smiles, the kind that had been absent from Pete and the rest of the men. Their chattering voices froze when they saw Nick and Jimmy.

"It's okay, boys," Pete said in English. "They are friends. They will be staying here tonight."

The pre-teen looking boys regained their ear-to-ear grins and started hooting and hollering as they raced back to camp, presumably to spread the news.

When the gang of men reached the village, the sun was as low as it would get this time of year. Nick knew it must be late. He wondered how these people lived. If they had set bedtimes like townspeople or if they were free to set their own clocks the way he and his brother had been doing all summer.

Nick could only see the village dimly, but he could make out several shelters. What surprised him most was how modern, even Western, the building materials looked.

Pete stood beside him, taking a more active role as his and Jimmy's escort. The expression on Nick's face must have been obvious.

"What were you expecting? Teepees and igloos?" Pete asked.

"No," Nick blurted. "Well, maybe something like that."

Pete smiled again. "We don't see many outsiders here, but we make use of what resources we do have, and some of it comes from town."

Nick could see the primary building materials were cinder blocks. But they had bermed the homes with earth on three sides, a necessary strategy for surviving the winters this far north.

About twenty similarly sized shelters peppered the landscape. Some were clumped close together; some weren't. Nick imagined they'd been built over a long period of time, as needed, and with no long-term shape or design in mind. This was no subdivision. This was how people lived when there was no perceived scarcity of land and when you belonged to a community or tribe, not just a so-called nuclear family unit.

"Are these all houses?" Nick asked.

"Most are. We have a couple of buildings for storage. And a smokehouse. The rest are places for people to sleep."

The ground was soft but well worn, Nick noticed as they traveled into the center of the village. There was no need to mow grass here. The distinction between path and lawn was ambiguous. There were obvious, clearly worn trails where no grass grew. Then there were many in-between places, where foot traffic limited the growth but allowed some green things to emerge and survive. No central planners here, Nick decided. No neighborhood covenants or housing restrictions. No one to tell you that you couldn't leave your garage door open to the road. No one to tell you your lawn was overgrown or that you couldn't use a certain color of roofing.

The pre-teens returned bringing along with them more children of various ages. Then adults started coming out to lay eyes on the visitors. Some came out of shelters. Most were already congregated outside near the center of the village where a large fire roared.

The fire was bright enough to compete with the near-horizon sun's intensity. Nick's eyes reacted, his pupils narrowing. And the people on either side of the fire seemed to fade into the darker surroundings. Nick didn't care for the crowds, even this one out in the wilderness. He was lost for a moment, staring into the shadows beside and behind the fire. It made him feel safe. It made him feel far away from his discomfort and from the world he had left.

An image emerged from the darkness. A face. Eyes as dark as the night and hair to match. A beautiful girl walked from beside the fire and headed toward them.

"This is my daughter," Pete said, holding out a hand toward the girl.

She seemed to glide toward them like she didn't have to move her feet. She embraced her father's one-armed hug and maintained her gaze at Nick and Jimmy. She didn't smile—perhaps a family trait, Nick thought—but she didn't seem unfriendly either.

"I'm Lusa," she said holding her hand out to Nick.

"Nick," he said, gently shaking her soft hand. "And this is my younger brother Jimmy." Jimmy gave a shy half-wave.

"It means midnight," Pete said. Nick's dubious expression prompted more explanation. "Her name. Lusa means midnight. She was born at night on an evening much like this one." Pete looked up as if he was breathing in the night itself. The wind blew gently through the tops of nearby trees.

"Beautiful," Nick said reflexively.

The girl's eyes widened and Pete stiffened.

"I mean, Lusa's beautiful. The name. Well . . . you're beautiful too. But I meant . . ."

Finally, Pete and Lusa both broke into laughter. Then Pete slapped Nick a little too hard on the back and said, "Let's get something to eat."

As they approached the fire, Nick noticed the outdoor hearth was connected to an oven out of which something delicious wafted his way. And to one side of the fire pit was a metal rod, mostly rusted from constant heating, that held what was left of an animal's carcass that had been roasted over the fire. It had been picked over already by the rest of the tribe. Nick couldn't tell what kind of animal it was (it had been a huge hunk of meat to start with), but the combination of smells from baked and roasted foods was too inviting to allow for squeamish or selective thoughts. Whatever it was, Nick decided, it couldn't be too bad, or the rest of the villagers wouldn't have eaten it.

"Sit here," Pete said pointing to two boulders near the hearth. Nick felt conspicuous using them; many of the villagers sat on the ground nearby making these prime seats literal pedestals. He wasn't sure if Pete was being gracious giving them the choice seats or if he put them there so the rest of the village could observe them.

Nick watched as Pete walked over to some of the older men, men that hadn't been in the hunting party. Pete spoke in his native tongue and occasionally gestured with his hands toward Nick and Jimmy. He was talking about them, Nick knew. He was explaining why on earth he'd brought back two white kids, why they'd be spending the night and eating their food.

"How old are you?" a pre-teen boy asked. Nick and Jimmy both swiveled on their seats and found that a half-dozen kids had congregated to their backsides.

"Me or him?" Jimmy asked.

A younger girl said, "You," as if she was picking Jimmy for some game.

"I'm sixteen. He's a year-and-a-half older than me."

"Told you," said another girl who shoved a chubby boy. The boy reacted but spoke in his own language. The kids turned to look at Jimmy—it was clear they wanted to deal with who was younger, closer to their age—to see if he was offended by them not speaking in English.

Jimmy seemed to pick up on this and raised his hands to calm the children. Then he did his impression of the chubby boy sounding like something straight out of Disney's old Peter Pan cartoon. "Me-han-a-te-tanaha."

The kids erupted in laughter. Jimmy obviously butchered their language, but they seemed relieved they could kid with one of them.

"Nick," a soft voice said fireside.

Nick turned and saw Lusa holding two bowls of food for them. "Thank you," Nick said grabbing his.

Jimmy didn't seem to notice, continuing to play with the kids.

"Jimmy," Nick said digging an elbow into his side. Jimmy turned slowly, pretending the dig didn't hurt and trying to show his new audience he wasn't being bossed around by his big brother.

"Ah, food!" Jimmy said animatedly, and the kids behind him laughed again at their new-found clown. Nick had seen this before. Jimmy related better with younger kids. Teenagers his own age saw his weakness, recognized his lowly place in the pecking order. But young ones—all they saw was this overgrown kid, a fellow spirit donning a near grown-up physique: every child's fantasy.

"I hope you like it," Lusa said to Nick.

"After the day we've had," Jimmy answered, still performing for the children, "I'd eat a horse." The kids laughed again. Nick knew it almost didn't matter what Jimmy said. They would find it funny as long as he played along and acted a fool.

Nick looked up at Lusa who stood before them. She wore blue jeans with a thinly knit blouse. The only traditional looking clothing she wore was her leather shoes and a necklace.

Nick scooted over on his rock. "Won't you join us?"

"Oh, no. I can't," she said in such a way that Nick realized he had asked her to do something inappropriate, something that would embarrass her.

"I just didn't want to make you stand," he said.

She smiled warmly. "Do you want me to go?"

"No, I just—"

"Is it good?" Lusa interrupted. Nick was glad she had. He sensed he was getting into an awkward conversation. He paused and took a bite of the meat using bare hands sans utensils. It was fall-off-the-bone tender and, although it didn't have any noticeable spices on it, was the best tasting meat he could remember eating. Before his mouthful was swallowed, he added a big bite of bread to the mix. He couldn't see much about the food he was eating—too dark. The bread, like the meat, was plain but hearty.

"Best I've had in ages," he said magnanimously.

She smiled, pleased. "I'll be right back," she said as she turned and disappeared beyond the fire.

Nick enjoyed his feast in a bowl. As he chewed, he slowed to appreciate the moment. The bowl appeared hand-made and undoubtedly was. The bread was excellent, and he couldn't decide which of the two foods delighted his senses more. They were the first warm foods he'd eaten in nearly a week, and they made him feel like a new man.

He listened to Jimmy continue to entertain the children behind them. And although he and his brother were strangers here, Nick felt a sense of calm peace flood over him. He was safe. He was with people who at least tolerated him; some welcomed him. His brother had found an audience, and he had found Lusa. It didn't matter how premature his feelings were. He felt them now, and he hadn't felt anything like this since long before the update. For this moment, he was entirely satisfied.

"Here you are," Lusa said returning with cups of water.

Nick thanked her and downed almost the whole cup, holding half of it in his mouth with puffed out cheeks. Her reaction caused him to fight the instinct to laugh, and he struggled, almost choking on the large gulp. "What was that for?" he asked playfully.

Lusa just smiled, not seeming to know what to say. Then as if some invisible bell had sounded, she said, "Well, I'll see you tomorrow. Bye."

He watched as she walked to a group of women to the right of the fire, close to the hearth. Nick noticed that except for the children behind him, the men and women kept mostly separate from each other. He wondered how much of this was just people being with those they like to be with and how much was some social norm that he was oblivious to.

As if on cue, Pete came back and sat on the rock that Jimmy had been using (Jimmy was gone, probably still playing with the kids).

174

Before Pete could say anything, Nick spoke. "I hope it's okay for my brother to be with the children."

Pete's expression was one of confusion. "Why wouldn't it be? He seems like a big kid himself."

"He is. I just didn't want to make anyone uncomfortable. I realize we're visitors here, but Jimmy doesn't always think about his situation. Sometimes he just acts at an emotional level—doesn't keep his head."

Pete listened and continued his pose after Nick finished speaking, still looking like he was taking the information in. "Well, at least you know what you get with him. He's not pretending."

"You can say that again. He feels it. Whatever he does or says, it's from deep within."

"But not with you?"

Now it was Nick's turn to pause. "Let's just say, I like to make decisions more slowly. Pete," he said changing the subject, "thank you for helping us. I don't know what we'd be doing right now if you hadn't found us."

"Oh, you seem pretty resourceful. You made it this far. I think you would have found a way to Deadhorse."

"I don't know. I do know tonight wouldn't have been spent like this." He raised his cup and bowl towards the fire and people, expressing his appreciation.

"Are you finished with those?"

Nick nodded.

175

Pete took the bowl and cup from him, but then returned the cup. "Better hang on to that." Pete turned. "Lusa," he yelled. His elevated voice seemed out of place in the midst of such a tranquil, amiable environment. But few heads turned, and no one seemed alarmed.

Nick watched as Lusa came to fetch Nick and Jimmy's empty bowls. She made one quick glance at Nick, then kept her eyes faithfully on her father. "Thank you, my dear," Pete said as she left. Then, like performing a magic trick, Pete pulled a clear glass bottle out from behind him. It had no label and its contents looked like water. Pete poured a small sip into his cup, then held out the bottle to Nick.

"What is it?" Nick asked.

"The good stuff. Just take a little."

Nick complied, taking an equal amount to what Pete had poured. Pete waited for Nick, and when they were both ready, they took sips, locking eyes the whole time.

The liquid poured into Nick's mouth easily and rushed to the back of his throat, somehow faster than water should travel. It was only by the time he tried to swallow that the burning—the incredible lining-of-your-nose destroying sensation—kicked in. Nick saw Pete's eyes widen. It didn't look like it was from the same surprise Nick was experiencing but from amusement.

Nick swallowed hard, then coughed up a lung. "What was that?"

"I told you. The good stuff."

It was up to Nick to realize they were drinking whisky. It had to be. Unless Pete had gone broke and was trying to poison him, nothing else fit the bill. Nick tried to regain his composure. He'd had a sip of his dad's Coors Light before, discovered it was disgusting, and hadn't been interested in trying alcohol again. But tonight, what he and Pete were doing, it didn't feel like something Jimmy would get into. It didn't seem like kids breaking into the liquor cabinet and getting drunk while their parents were away on vacation. This was about something. This meant something. He could tell it in the way Pete was behaving, the way Pete was sitting close to him. They were connecting. Pete was trying to bring Nick into a bond that he didn't fully grasp.

"More slowly this time," Pete said as he held out the bottle again. Nick took the imbibement with the respect it deserved. If he was to get drunk, it wasn't so he could party and lose control. He was with someone he wanted to impress, wanted to make like him, even.

Nick took a small sip. This time the burn wasn't such a surprise and the cell membranes in his mouth, throat, and nose were partly desensitized from the fire-on-skin effect.

Nick looked around at the village: the fire, the cabins, the forest edge surrounding them, the people being together, the children. "This is a wonderful place," he finally said almost by accident.

"I'm glad you like it. Did you enjoy the caribou?"

"So that's what that was. Yes. Best steak I remember eating. But I'm a little confused."

Pete turned his head slightly as if bracing for criticism.

"Where'd the bread come from?"

"The oven," Pete said pointing.

"No, I mean, wheat doesn't grow around here, does it?"

"Oh," Pete relaxed. Almost grinned. "You know white people aren't the only ones that know how to buy and sell." Nick could tell by the way he said it Pete wasn't offended. "We sell some of our skins and furs and buy flour with the money we make. Sometimes we have to buy block for new houses or lamp oil or clothes. Stuff like that. But for the most part, we don't need those things. They're just convenient."

Nick listened. It seemed like Pete was reciting practiced speech, something he had told or expected to tell the rest of his people. "Was the update very hard for your village?" Nick asked.

"Yes," Pete said sharply. Apparently, Nick had struck a nerve.

Nick tried to do damage control. "I don't mean to pry. You know, Jimmy and I lost everything. Everyone we know but each other. This place—it just seems untouched. Pristine even."

"Well, it's not," Pete said. "There were losses. We lost good people." Nick was stunned, and it must have shown on his face. "Yes, several people were using the DataMind app here. You probably are wondering why anyone would need it here. I asked the same thing, but people—young people—were hooked on their phones before DataMind ever came out. And they jumped on it like flies to honey."

"Young people?" Nick questioned. "I thought you had to be eighteen years old or older to use DataMind. That's why me and my brother weren't affected."

"Yeah, that's how it's supposed to work. But therein lies the problem. The phones are a technology that we older people have little use for. For whatever reason the kids…" He stopped to control himself. He took the rest of his whisky. "My son among them— they thought that they needed to be online. They could barely even get a cell signal up here, and since we wouldn't let them run our generators, they had to use those silly solar chargers that took half a day to charge. But they begged and begged to use data on their phones. At some point we didn't want to hear it anymore and gave in. Some of us did. Some of us didn't."

Nick took another sip. He wanted to say he was sorry about Pete's son, but he didn't feel like his condolence could be taken seriously. He hadn't known the kid. It would seem trite and insincere. "What about Lusa? She's young."

"Yes, she is. Some kids listen to their parents, and some don't. Simple as that." Pete poured another glass, this one taller than the last. Nick did the same albeit he wasn't ready for as tall a pour.

The two sat sipping their drinks silently. But the silence didn't feel awkward to Nick. It felt like they were both exactly where they wanted to be. Nick looked at the fire. It had dimmed a bit, but he knew it would probably burn for several more hours. Behind it must be west, he thought, because the evening sun hung on the horizon there. He could barely see it due to the trees, but there was a break in the forest growth where the gooey, orange sun broke through, promising it wasn't really gone and that it would be there waiting for them until tomorrow when it would ascend high into the sky.

"Listen, Nick," Pete said breaking the peaceful quiet. "I spoke with some of the elders." His eyes glanced toward where several men were clumped together. "They don't think it was by accident you and Jimmy came here."

A rush of thoughts flooded Nick's one-hundred-proof brain. "We didn't come here on purpose. I mean, if our tire hadn't blown, we would have never even known you existed."

"That's not what I mean. Not what they mean. They think you were brought to us for a purpose. They think the Spirits, the Universe, brought you here."

Nick blinked. "They're saying God blew out my tire?"

Pete grinned, showing big white teeth. "You're as skeptical as me." His smile faded. "Like I said before, we lost people. Good people to the update. The elders say the universe always seeks balance. That's even why the world went broke in the first place: too out of balance. But our people and our ancestors, we've sought to live in balance with nature for ages. For as long as our people have lived in this place. So, the elders believe you and Jimmy may be the universe's attempt to rebalance us, to give us back part of what we lost."

Nick was struck by the magnitude of Pete's words. "I don't know what to say. I'm grateful, but you barely know us."

"That's what I said." Another grin. "But they are seers. Or they think that they are, and who am I to tell them they're not. Although, it would have been helpful if they had foreseen the update. But I guess it doesn't work that way." Pete's words could have taken on a sarcastic tone but didn't. For him, whatever religion, magic, hooey the seers had—it was real.

Pete and Nick finished another pour of whisky. Not having drunk much before, Nick wasn't sure if this was considered being drunk. He knew the law had an empirical line, a blood alcohol level, that they counted as the point at which you couldn't legally drive. But how would he know where that invisible line was? All he knew was that everything was fine except when he got up to pee. Then it felt like his feet were a hundred yards away from his head. His appendages transmitted nervous signals via radio waves to and from his brain, which had a little man inside manually pulling levers to operate the machine called his body.

Pete pointed him to a set of bushes beyond the little creek. Crossing the creek was harder than it looked. It wasn't, however, due to his hesitation. In fact, his whisky induced ten-foot-tall self-image told him he could easily leap across. When he tried, he splashed loudly with both feet in the water, a foot from the far bank. He twisted his left foot on the creek-bottom rocks.

He'd feel that in the morning, he told himself. He knew it had happened, but he hadn't felt any pain. He wondered if he'd even remember how he'd gotten the sore ankle.

After Nick returned to the fire, he noticed Pete hadn't slowed down on the drink. The bottle—if he was remembering correctly—was markedly emptier than the last time Nick had seen it. He felt guilty for his thoughts: the stereotypical Redman drunk on firewater. He knew better, but he also didn't have the faculties to suppress this type of thought, the kind that he could sometimes push down and forget he ever thought it.

Pete looked up slowly as Nick sat down, almost like Pete had totally forgotten about him. A delayed reaction. "There you are," Pete said hoarsely.

"There I am," Nick echoed. Another pour to Nick. He felt obliged to receive it, but his walk demonstrated he'd had enough. He felt really good and told himself this was the last pour.

"Nick, don't worry too much about what I told you. You and Jimmy have had enough on your shoulders. You don't need my burden too."

So, he's a sad drunk, Nick's demon-on-his-shoulder whispered. "Are you kidding? You've taken a huge weight off of us, even if it's temporary. This is the best I've felt since long before the update. And Jimmy—I have no idea where he is—but he's having a blast. This is great for him too."

"All I'm saying is you don't have to leave in the morning. You can stay longer. The elders say so, and I say so. Deadhorse isn't going anywhere, and you're

183

closer to it than Fairbanks. I'd say you're less than a day's drive away. We'll help you with the tire when you want to go, even fill your tank back up with gas. But you don't have to leave. And you certainly don't have to go tomorrow. You could wait a month, and the weather would still be good. You'd make it easy before the snow starts coming hard."

Nick smiled in appreciation. "I'll think about it," was all that came out. He finished his drink and stood up. Pete gave the same slow response looking up at him.

"Pete?"

"Yeah."

"Where do I sleep tonight?"

Pete pointed at the same bushes beyond the creek that Nick had visited earlier, waited for effect, then burst into loud laughter. It was alarming how loud he laughed at his own joke, and Nick found himself following suit. Not because he thought it was a hysterical joke but because of Pete's reaction.

When the hoots and hollers subsided, Pete pointed at one of the cabins with a solemn expression. "That one's empty now. Use it."

Nick nodded in appreciation. As he walked to the cinder block cabin, he noticed it was different from most of the cabins in that the lamp that hung outside on an Indian's version of a porch was unlit. He took the lamp off its hanger and stared at it dumbly. Then he noticed a large box of matches in the single window by the door. He lit the lamp with ease having practiced plenty back at Grandpa Joe's basement.

He pushed open the heavy wooden door. It seemed to weigh a ton, but it glided open smoothly. Or, at least, that's how it seemed to Nick. Inside, Nick looked around. The lamp's barrel was so dirty it barely threw light to the nearest wall. He was surprised by what he saw. He didn't know why. More teepees and igloos, he told himself. He had such a naïve, romantic view of how these people were supposed to live that the bed on a frame, desk, and chair surprised him.

He made his way to the bed with the last bit of steam left inside him—the little man in his head sweating hard to pull the heavy levers that were bogging down more and more by the second. He set the lamp down on the floor and collapsed onto the empty bed, not caring whose it had been, whether it was dirty. Nothing.

He closed his eyes, then flashed them open in as much panic as his ethanol-soaked mind could muster. He pushed his body over the edge of the bed, headfirst, and blew wildly toward the lamp. Somehow, he blew it out with one breath.

He rolled himself back onto the bed and closed his eyes. He felt himself sink deeply into the bedding like it was velvet quicksand.

185

Fleeting thoughts across the movie screen of his mind. His mom and dad. His stepmother. Jimmy playing with the kids. *Where was Jimmy?* It didn't matter. He'd find some place to sleep. Someone would tell him what to do.

Then he found the one. The thought that he liked the most and the one he wanted to hold onto until he fell asleep. Lusa.

CHAPTER 18

NICK WOKE UP in a way he couldn't remember waking in years: slowly. Usually he was hearing the alarm clock for school, or his parents would wake him in the summer: "Wakey, wakey, eggs and bakey," his stepmom used to say after she had already been up since five a.m., hyped on her latest DataMind meditation session. "Early bird gets the worm," she'd add. And before DataMind, he had Jimmy who liked to sleep in as much as he did. But if Jimmy happened to be the first one up, he would start shoving Nick over and over, shaking him awake. That was the way it had been back in Fairbanks before the update, before moving into Grandpa Joe's basement, and before driving two-hundred miles toward Deadhorse in a worn-out, flat-tired, seen-better-days Dodge Ram van.

Today was different. The single window to the left of the door allowed warm light into the cabin, first hitting the wall and gently shifting its angle to strike

Nick in bed. It was like so many morning glories who waited for the sun to invite them to open their petals. It was how it was supposed to be. Nick felt the sunshine welcome him back from the underworld of sleep. He breathed deeply and enjoyed the silence. The world was ugly, unsafe. But he was in the safest place he could imagine: a village high in virgin forest with clean water, good people, and a way of life that sounded better than anything he'd seen his mom and dad experience.

He sat up and remembered as much of the previous night as he could. Pete had told him he didn't have to leave. He wasn't sure what he'd do, but he didn't feel like he was in any kind of hurry now. This had been the first break in the life-or-death tension he'd felt for the last week. And he wasn't keen on getting back into the ring again, not after he'd been beaten up so many times. This place was nice, and he was going to enjoy it while it lasted.

He'd need to find Jimmy and talk to him about staying, but he knew his little brother—as much as he had been the one wanting to go to Deadhorse—wasn't chomping at the bit, ready to go. He doubted he was even awake yet. And if he was, he was probably playing with those kids, oblivious to the larger world around him.

Nick stood and approached the door. Nothing makes you need to pee more than a night of drinking, he realized for the first time in his life. But something on the wall caught his eye. It was a photograph of a teenage boy and Pete with a truck bed full of furs and skins. They were smiling ear to ear, and Pete had his arm around the kid's shoulder.

Another picture beside it had the boy and several other people Nick didn't recognize, but there was Pete and Lusa.

"Family," Nick said out loud. This guy was related to Pete and Lusa. He turned around and looked at the stoic room. Few belongings. Some clothes. A rifle in the corner. Not much to go on, but Nick didn't need more clues. He remembered Pete's words and expression last night. This cabin belonged to Pete's son, or it used to belong to him.

A cold chill went down Nick's back. Then he exhaled, releasing a mournful sentiment. Poor Pete, he thought.

As he exited the cabin, the smell of cooking greeted him. He breathed it in and headed back toward the center of the village where the fire had burned last night.

He didn't know what time it was, but by the looks of things he was late to the party. The whole village seemed to be out, and most people were nearly finished eating. He wondered what would be on the menu. Bacon and eggs would hit the spot, but that probably wasn't an option. He hadn't noticed any refrigeration or even electricity for that matter, although Pete had mentioned generators and solar chargers.

As he reached the hearth, he felt the warmth of the outdoor oven radiating. Lusa greeted him, "Hey, sleepy head."

"My alarm clock didn't go off," he said smiling.

Lusa gave him one of the same kinds of hand-made bowls he'd used last night. In it was simple fare: some kind of dark blue berries he didn't recognize and a large biscuit. But he was glad for it.

"You eat biscuits, don't you?" she asked.

"They're my favorite," Nick lied. What did it matter? He'd eat anything if he was hungry, and hot food beat cold cereal and spam any day.

"In the colder months, we often have meat available for most meals," she explained. "The caribou keep well in the freezing temperatures, but in the summer, we have to hurry to finish an animal."

Nick took a big bite and nodded in understanding. He sat down on the ground near the hearth. He was glad he wasn't put on the rocks like he was last night. It had almost felt like he was in time-out, detention even. Lusa started to return to a different group. Nick thought quickly.

"Hey, there's something I don't get."

"What's that?" she said looking coy.

"Can't you just hang meat in your smokehouse? Wouldn't that keep things through the summer?"

Lusa's eyes widened, then relaxed with a gentle smile. "It's not that kind of smokehouse," she said. "I've got to do some chores. See you later?"

"Yeah, okay."

That was weird, he thought. He must have said something wrong, or maybe she's telling the truth and really had to go.

Nick watched the children playing. It was some variation on red-light, green-light with a different language and hand signals. And somehow the dogs were involved. Jimmy wasn't with them.

"You sleep alright?" Pete asked, approaching him from behind.

Nick hurried to swallow the mouthful of biscuit. "Like a baby," he said. "Say, I'm surprised you got up before I did. We were going pretty hard last night, and I gave up before you did."

Pete was less animated than last night, more like he was out near the pipeline. "I'm an old-timer. Lots of practice." He gave only a hint of a smile that was held more in the glimmer of his eyes than the rest of his face.

"Have you seen Jimmy?" Nick asked.

Pete shook his head, then titled it toward the children. "Ask them."

Nick's relaxed calm was quickly dissipating with each passing moment, each time he looked for Jimmy unsuccessfully.

"After you find your brother, do you plan to stay here?" Pete asked matter-of-factly.

"I would like to. At least a while longer. But I need to talk to Jimmy about it."

"Well, when you do—if we haven't left yet—you're welcome to come with some of the men. We're going to walk part of our territory, make sure there aren't any…" He stopped himself and looked at the children. "Make sure everything's safe."

Nick understood they were going on patrol, looking for crazies.

"I'll come find you," Nick said, "after I get Jimmy."

Pete walked off with little reaction. It was peculiar to Nick that Pete could seem so different this morning than he did last night. It wasn't that he was two-faced, a dishonest scoundrel who didn't show his cards. Pete was a straight shooter. But he was so guarded now. It wasn't until his day was done and his lips touched the bottle that the fun-loving, gregarious Pete emerged. Nick wondered if he'd always been this way or whether losing his son had done it to him.

He stood and drifted over to the children nearby. One of the dogs turned and growled at the outsider. "No!" yelled a little girl who commenced to speak commands to the dog in her native language. The dog heeled but kept its eye on Nick.

"Hey, thanks. You saved my life just then," Nick teased the girl.

She stared back with a smile that seemed smashed together like she was forcibly holding back showing her teeth.

"Have you seen my brother?"

"You mean Jimmy?" a chubby boy interjected.

Nick waited for the answer, but then realized how kids don't really use rhetorical questions. "Yeah, Jimmy. Have you seen him?"

"He was going to spend the night at my house," the chubby kid said, "but he went to the smokehouse last night and never came out."

"Where?" Nick asked quickly.

The gang of little ones all raised their arms and pointed to the small cabin higher up the gentle rolling hill. It was the furthest away from camp and wasn't bermed with earth the way all the rest were.

"Thanks, guys," Nick said as he started toward the cabin. Nick's mind raced as he climbed the subtle incline. He found himself walking faster and faster as he neared the cabin. His first reaction to the children's words was to think back to the garage, Jimmy's suicide attempt. Except, that didn't make sense. Jimmy hadn't made enough noise. He hadn't done something overtly obvious to draw attention to himself. Unless, Nick thought, he was serious this time and didn't want to be stopped.

Nick was nearly in a dead run when he reached the cabin. He grabbed the door handle—he didn't knock, and, apparently, there were no locks in the village anyway—and yanked open the door.

He was met by a cloud of smoke that eagerly billowed out the entranceway. Nick coughed and waived his hand in front of his face, trying to clear the air.

"Jimmy!" he yelled, entering the opaque room.

"Hey, Nick. What are you doing here?" his brother answered with a weird, bubbly sound in his voice.

The smoke cleared a bit, and Nick's eyes adjusted to the darker room. There he saw Jimmy sitting on the earthen floor in the middle of the room. On each side of him were four little bowls, not too dissimilar from the ones Nick had eaten from. But in the place of food were ashes, embers, and rising smoke.

"What are you doing?" Nick asked as he jerked his brother upright, pulling him by one arm.

Jimmy stood but seemed untouched by this rough treatment. "This is the smokehouse. Isn't it great?"

Jimmy was acting strange, even for Jimmy. Nick looked around the room expecting to see something resembling sides-of-beef hanging from the rafters. There were rafters, and things were hanging. But they weren't pieces of meat.

Nick moved to touch one. It was dry like old, brittle paper. The green-brown material was twisted and braided together, tied at the top to the lateral beams spanning the room's width.

"It's a cornucopia. A Shangri-La," Jimmy pronounced.

Nick peered at the walls and saw what must have been ceremonial art: a collage of animal bones, feathers, strung beads, and paint. But much to his horror, several objects had fallen to the floor and were in pieces.

"What'd you do?" he demanded.

Jimmy merely shrugged, deflecting Nick's accusation. Then it hit Nick: first the effect of the smoke, and then what it all meant. He was feeling high. It wasn't like the whisky exactly, but his mind was being altered.

He grabbed Jimmy by the arm again and dragged him out of the cabin. His lungs cleared, and slowly he felt the effects of the marijuana dissipate from his mind and body.

He looked at Jimmy. "How long have you been in there?"

"The whole time, big brother." Jimmy beamed a Cheshire cat grin with squinty eyes.

"All night?"

Jimmy shrugged honestly. "I guess."

"Come on."

Nick half-dragged, half-pushed his brother down the hillside into the village. About halfway down, the children came running to them.

"Jimmy," shouted the chubby boy. They grabbed hold of him like he was their prophet, like they could absorb his power if they could just get hold of him.

"Hey, guys," Jimmy said.

"Don't talk," Nick demanded.

"Don't talk?" Jimmy parroted.

"You heard me. Keep it sealed. I mean it." Nick paused from walking long enough to look at his brother and relay the seriousness of what he was saying. Jimmy was stoned out of his mind, but Nick intended to keep that a secret for as long as he could.

"Okay, but—"

"Eh! Not a word," Nick said cutting him off.

They resumed their descent, the children still clinging to their savior but receiving none of his charismatic words and certainly none of his magic. When they reached the hearth, Nick sat Jimmy down at one of the big rocks and told him not to move a muscle. Again, the serious tone and face was used to make it stick, to make Jimmy stick.

Lusa noticed Nick looking around the campground. "What is it?" she asked.

"Your dad. Where is he?"

Lusa pointed to a group of men walking away from camp. They'd already crossed the creek and were about to disappear into the tree line.

Nick took off after them. He reached the stream and leaped across it. He cleared it, but his left ankle landed hard and a surprising hot pain shot up his leg. That didn't make sense. He couldn't remember hurting himself, but there it was anyway: a tender ankle he'd have to nurse.

The men heard the sound of Nick's Olympian leap followed by his wincing and turned to greet their strange guest.

"Pete. We need to talk," Nick said out of breath.

Pete emerged from the group of men, much like he had at the pipeline. "What is it Nick?"

"I can't stay. We have to go. Today."

"I don't understand. There's no need for you—"

"I don't expect you to understand. But we have to go right now."

A pause as Pete ruminated. "You don't need my permission."

"I know, but we do need your help. We still have that flat tire, and you mentioned some tools."

Pete looked at his men and gave them the signal to go on without him. "Come. I'll get it for you."

197

The two returned to the village. Nick was anxious to get this over with, and he was equally nervous about keeping Jimmy quiet. To his relief, Jimmy was exactly where he'd left him. The kids had moved on, probably getting bored by the mime on a rock. Jimmy had his eyes closed and his arms extended. The sun was hitting him directly—it must be nearly noon—and he looked as if he was absorbing the sun's powers, charging his own batteries, or maybe he thought he was a plant trying to grow. As peculiar as it looked, at least he was quiet and still, Nick thought. He might get the two of them out of here before they realized what Jimmy had done.

"Wait here," Pete said.

Nick watched Pete go toward the smokehouse. Every alarm and siren internally began sounding. *Don't go in there. No, no, no, please. Don't look in there.*

His panic was all for naught, because Pete detoured to the right about thirty paces before reaching the smokehouse, entering what must have been a different utility building. It was only then that Nick noticed the radio tower and antenna beside the building.

Nick looked around the fire pit area. It was the least crowded he had seen it. Breakfast was over, and everyone seemed to have things they should be doing. Lusa was there. She was working too, cleaning the more-clay-than-brick oven after it had cooled.

She noticed him and looked away. It made Nick feel lousy. He wanted to talk with her again, one last time. Was she giving him the cold shoulder? Did she know he was leaving? Or was she just shy?

She finished whatever it was she was doing and took her bucket and brush and walked away, up toward a nearby cabin.

That was no accident, Nick thought. She kept her back to me. She didn't want to make eye contact, didn't want to speak. What did it matter now? She was someone he'd never see again. Ever. She belonged to the long list of friends, family, teachers, neighbors, and crushes that were gone. Another loss due to the update.

He turned and looked at his brother. *Correction*, he told himself, *another loss due to Jimmy being a totally unreliable junky wannabe*. First, they'd lost their place in Fairbanks because of his stupidity. And now, after finding a place that could actually support a meaningful life, a place for Jimmy to grow up and become a man— he had ruined it. Nick felt like taking the world's biggest sucker punch at his brother who still had his eyes closed. It would feel so good just to lay him out cold. Maybe even a bloody nose and black eye to boot.

"Here we go," Pete said carrying a black metal object in one hand and red gas can in the other.

"What's that?" Nick asked. He saw out of the corner of his eye Jimmy awaken, but he said nothing.

"A bottle jack," Pete answered. "It should be the right height for your van. It's kind of hard to tell without measuring it first."

Nick started to reach for the tool, ready to thank Pete for his hospitality and for letting him borrow the tool. But then he had a flash of awareness. "How do I get this back to you?"

"Actually," Pete corrected, "the right question is how do you get to the van? Did you memorize how we got to the village?"

Nick almost slapped his forehead. "Oh, man. I didn't even think about that. I mean, I have a general idea of how we came in, but…"

"I bet you could find the Dalton, but if you were off by just a few degrees you could easily end up a half-day north or south of your van. And how would you know which way to walk from there?"

Nick felt stupid, an idiot for not anticipating these problems. When Pete's people had found them at the road, he'd just been grateful for someone's help. And after he got to the village—it was so inviting, he tried to forget all about the van and Deadhorse, let alone how to get back to them.

"I'll take you there," Pete said.

"Are you sure?"

"Yes, but you'll have to carry the jack and gas," Pete said, handing him the heavier-than-it-looked tool. Pete set the can down, then reached over and grabbed his rifle that was against the now-cool hearth. "Let's get a move on," he said.

Jimmy stood, looking like he had rubbed together the last two remaining synapses in his brain to accomplish the feat. Nick shoved the jack into Jimmy's hands. "Here. This is for you." Then Nick picked up the gas can. He thought about swapping it with Jimmy for the jack—make Jimmy carry the five gallons back—but he decided it wasn't worth the risk of catching resistance from his brother.

The walk back was quiet. But it wasn't peaceful. Not for Nick, anyway. Sure, the world around them was pristine, tranquil. But inside, Nick was brooding. Fuming with anxiety and anger. He didn't want to be in this boat. He didn't want to be stuck with Jimmy. And, even though there was little reason to feel this way, he didn't want to leave Lusa.

A silver lining—as pathetic as it was—was that Jimmy was so stoned out of his mind that he was both quiet and agreeable. Nick was convinced he could tell him to do anything—walk off a cliff, shoot himself, anything—and he would do it.

When they reached the pipeline, Nick started looking for the van. The highway looked like a little, thin crust of gray on the horizon, just barely visible above the hillside between it and the pipeline. Nick spotted the van, noticeably lower in the back from the flat tire.

"Well, at least it's still here," he said to nobody.

When they reached the van, Nick noticed the Springfield nine-millimeter and Jimmy's shotgun both lying on the ground right where they'd left them. No one had touched them, Nick realized. They were truly in the middle of nowhere. Nothing but them, caribou, a wolf-howl in the distance, and an occasional crazy just to keep them on their toes. Because life wasn't hard enough, Nick fussed.

Nick hated the sight of the van, even their guns. It was everything he had been all too glad to forget. But Jimmy had, yet again, ruined things. And even if Nick had gotten him sober and they had escaped detection regarding the smokehouse incident—it would just be a matter of time before it happened again. It or something like it.

Pete grabbed the jack out of Jimmy's hand without saying anything. Nick noticed how he moved with decisiveness, the kinds of motions that showed his real self. A real man. A father. Despite Pete's silence, Nick felt like Pete was trying to protect them, trying to help them one last time before they, the prodigal children, left him forever.

Nick set the gas can down and rolled the inflated tire over after Pete had unscrewed the lug nuts and removed the flat tire. "You're not going to need this anymore," Pete said as he discarded it on the side of the road. Nick stared at the tire lying on its side. It was yet another piece of his past, a remnant from Grandpa Joe's garage, gone.

After a few seconds of tightening, checking, and retightening the lugs, Pete said, "That ought to do it." He reached down and turned the jack key and released the pressure. The van dropped down and caught itself with the support of the new tire. It had worked.

With reluctance, Nick picked up his Springfield, checked it, and tucked it in his waistline behind him. He knew better than to hand Jimmy the shotgun but instead placed it into the van. Its door was still open. Nick had a bad thought: what if an automatic light was on and the battery was dead?

Nick ran around to the driver's seat and turned on the keys that were still in the ignition. The van roared to life like an old curmudgeon being awakened from a mid-afternoon nap. It didn't want to run, but it did. Angrily.

Jimmy climbed into the back sheepishly. Pete opened the passenger side door and placed the jack in the floorboard.

"What's that for?" Nick asked.

"You may need it again, more than we will," Pete answered. Then he hefted the gas can and placed it beside the jack. "You'll need this too before you get to Deadhorse."

There was a long pause, and Pete looked Nick in the eyes. Nick felt like he could read his thoughts, could hear the regrets Pete felt but would never utter. He'd lost his son, and now he was losing his second chance. Unable to match his gaze or intensity, Nick looked away. He stuck his head out the door and peered up at the sun as if he was determining what time it was.

"You better get going," Pete said. "Deadhorse is one-hundred eighty miles north. How's your tank?"

Nick checked. "Half full."

"Then that extra can should do it. Go straight there. Don't slow down. Don't take more chances than you have to. And if you can't find this . . . what's his name?"

"Bob!" Jimmy belted out from the backseat.

Pete gave a confused look toward Jimmy but kept on going. "…Bob. If you can't find Bob, you have a place with us. Just don't wait until the snow starts to fall. It'll be too late. The road will be impassible then." Nick nodded, understanding.

Pete seemed to sense he was staying too long at the dance. He looked down, then backed up. He said nothing as he closed the door, turned and walked away.

DEADHORSE

CHAPTER 19

THE DRIVE NORTH was a rough one. It wasn't just the engine that handled poorly; it was the bumpy road that increasingly resembled a third-world foot path with bits of gravel and broken asphalt thrown in. Nick pushed the van, feeling as if he couldn't experience another flat or more car trouble. Lightning couldn't strike twice. And he wanted to get this over with. The rest of the drive. Whatever was going to happen or not happen when they got to Deadhorse. All of it.

Fortunately for Nick, Jimmy had fallen asleep in the back of the van. Nick figured he had been up most of the night getting higher and higher and from a combined result of intoxication and sleep deprivation, he had collapsed.

As angry as Nick was at his brother, there were mixed emotions. Jimmy had come off anti-depressants cold turkey. It was to be expected he would act erratically. Nick still felt responsible for him. But his sense of duty was wearing thin. He told himself that he didn't ditch the village just because he was embarrassed by his brother's social infraction.   The villagers probably used that smokehouse in a similar fashion anyway. Maybe it was for more religious or spiritual pursuits rather than for recreation, but Nick didn't see much difference in the two. Just like the wheat, the marijuana was one more commodity Nick figured the village couldn't produce themselves and would soon have to live without.

Jimmy appeared to be the junky type when he slipped up like that, but was he really that different than the consciousness-altering mystic native who used mushrooms or LSD to break through the veil and look at the other side? The difference, Nick figured, was that the Indians had a way of doing things, a social code, that allowed purveyors of mystery to use marijuana but only in a certain socially acceptable way.

The world that Nick and Jimmy had left had its similar rules. Not just social codes but veritable laws with penalties including jail time. You could get drunk off your rocker on alcohol *if* you were over twenty-one *and* you didn't steal your booze *and* you stayed home and didn't drive *and* you didn't become violent or belligerent to your family or friends. Even marijuana was legal in certain states now, something that was once only allowed on the reservations where the natives made their own laws.

It wasn't the drugs or even the withdrawal from the antidepressants that really got Jimmy in trouble; it was the rules. So then, Nick wondered, why would things be better in Deadhorse? Because that was the reason Nick told himself he had left the village: *Jimmy couldn't stay there and needed to go to Deadhorse.* A certain terrified part of himself wondered if it wasn't just wishful thinking. Deadhorse was this place they had talked about, a place Jimmy wanted to go, a place that had Bob who was the only other person alive who still remembered Grandpa Joe, and it was the end of the world, the most northern post still inhabited by human beings. Tibet had the top of the world, but Deadhorse had the end of it.

So, why would this be different for Jimmy? Wouldn't he just screw up like always? Before the update, there had been safety nets, excuses, pills, and councilors who stroked his fragile ego. But now, mistakes had real consequences, and no one cared if you had an excuse. There was no reason to think that Deadhorse, perhaps the least habitable town in the world, would be any different. If anything, the consequences for stupidity would be worse there.

The reason, Nick told himself, that Jimmy would be better off in Deadhorse was containment. From what he remembered Bob saying—who knows if his memories were accurate after all the rambling conversations he and Jimmy had had about it—their destination was a research station with only one other resident. And it was far removed from the truck-stop called a town. Nick believed, if it was possible anywhere, he could tame and control his brother there. What could he possibly get into? And maybe, just maybe, Bob would represent some sort of grandfatherly influence, a word of wisdom that Jimmy desperately needed to heed.

"Where are we," Jimmy said from the back seat.

"Alaska," Nick answered.

Jimmy didn't go for his obvious ploy but instead crawled up into the front passenger seat.

"Welcome back to the world of reality, sleeping beauty."

"Shut up," Jimmy snapped.

A few moments passed as Jimmy appeared to still be regaining his faculties. Nick figured he'd let his brother do the explaining, when he was ready. He waited.

"What do we have to eat?" Jimmy finally asked.

"Same thing as always. Go look and see."

Jimmy crawled over the console and into the back of the van. The sounds that came up were like those Nick had heard camping in the Denali National Park when the bears would rummage through the garbage. The clanking stopped, and Jimmy returned with two cans of spam and a plastic fork.

"Good thing I grabbed this plastic ware back at the Wally's. Almost didn't think of it. Can you imagine how nasty it would be to eat this with your fingers?"

Nick didn't answer. It seemed pretty nasty with or without forks. Especially when Jimmy did it. He had a habit of slurping each bite regardless of the texture of the food. The slurps plus the drawn out smooshy cuts into the spam was all Nick could take. He knew it shouldn't matter, shouldn't bother him this badly, but it did. When Jimmy opened the second can and released a burp to mark the occasion, Nick spoke out. "Can't you do that somewhere else?"

"Uh, no," Jimmy quipped sarcastically. "Someone made us leave this awesome, pristine forest village where everyone was happy, had plenty of elbow room, and didn't have to live on spam."

Nick felt his face grow warm and the pressure built in his jaws. "Are you kidding?"

"Should I be?"

"You think that *I* decided to leave the village because I wanted to be stuck here with you?"

"I don't know why you did it, but no one asked me for my opinion."

"That's because you were a bumbling, incoherent idiot!" Nick pulled down his emotions, trying to keep them in check. He needed to keep them from jumping into the next higher gear, or he knew he would say more things he'd regret.

"They have a whole house for that stuff. You think they care that I smoke some? Come on," Jimmy said self-righteously.

"Jimmy," Nick said with extreme effort to remain calm, "I took us out because, if we'd stayed, they would have discovered all the pot you'd smoked and the stuff you'd smashed and would have thrown us out. Or worse."

"Worse? What, you think they would have killed us?"

"I don't know, but you ought to be thankful I was there to protect you. I bailed you out again. The least you can do is be grateful."

"You have some nerve," Jimmy retorted. Nick wasn't used to the sound in Jimmy's voice. It wasn't the same weak, passive tone that he expected. "You've been calling the shots this whole time. First, you said we weren't going to Deadhorse. Later, when you'd changed your mind, you decided to stop at Wally's and get us attacked by the King of the Hill. Then you decided to stop for gas, not where I suggested, and get us attacked yet again. Then you decided we should join an Indian village. Then you decided we leave. I'm getting sick and tired of you making all the decisions and not asking me first."

Nick swerved the van hard off the side of the road. The tires screeched and the top-heavy conversion van felt like it was going to tip over. Nick pumped the breaks and both boys, unbuckled, were pushed forward out of their seats.

"Get out of the car," Nick said as he opened his own door.

"What are you doing?"

"Get out." Nick walked around the front of the van and reached the passenger side door and yanked it open.

"Get out," Nick repeated, this time grabbing his brother by the arm and pulling.

Jimmy nearly fell to the ground but recovered and brushed his brother's hand off. "What's this about?"

"It ends now," Nick said. "Right now. All this crap. All these games. They're going to end now."

"Or what? You threatening me? You telling me what to do again? What a surprise!"

Nick grabbed Jimmy with both hands by his shirt and slammed him up against the side of the van. He felt saliva fly out of his mouth as he breathed hard in Jimmy's face. No words came out. Jimmy's eyes started to well up with tears and his cheek quivered.

"Oh, no you don't. You're not going to pull that stunt," Nick insisted. "You talk a big talk, but when you meet resistance, you turn into a babbling Nancy and cry for your mommy."

"Shut up!" Jimmy screamed, his voice wobbling with uncontrolled frequencies. He pushed Nick back.

Then he ran at him, head down, like the defensive lineman he'd never been.

Nick saw it coming but didn't feel threatened. He could handle Jimmy, or so he thought.

The younger and lighter weight brother slammed into Nick. Nick tried to stay upright and hold his ground against the pathetic attack. But to Nick's surprise, Jimmy had more power, more strength than he would have ever anticipated. The two boys fell to the ground, dust flying.

Nick felt sharp gravels dig into his side as they rolled on the uneven ground. Finally, Nick found himself on top, held his brother down with two hands, then released one and punched Jimmy in the nose.

Jimmy's head bounced back against the asphalt rubble. His eyes lost their focus for a moment.

When Nick saw the blood flowing profusely from Jimmy's almost certainly broken nose, he released his grip and rolled off his brother.

Jimmy squealed in legitimate agony.

Nick started to say that it served him right, but he stopped himself. Now, Nick realized, it was he instead of Jimmy that had crossed the line.

Jimmy tried to raise himself, to sit up. He alternated hands, trying to stop the bleeding. Looking like a newborn colt unsure of its limbs, he kept collapsing to the ground and trying again.

Nick got up and walked slowly to the van. He grabbed a roll of toilet paper, returned, and threw it underhand to Jimmy who had finally sat upright. Jimmy went to work trying to stop the bleeding.

Nick stood and scratched the dirt with his foot for a moment, then sat down and waited.

Neither boy looked at each other for some time. By the sound of it, Jimmy's nose had stopped bleeding. Or at least, Jimmy had stopped that gurgling, choke-on-your-own-blood routine.

Nick felt regret but knew he wasn't the only one wrong. Jimmy really was a piece of work, and the wallop that he'd received from Nick was nothing compared to what was waiting for him in the real world if he didn't get it together. Still, Nick felt like he'd lost his moral high ground. Like he'd blown it. Right or wrong, he didn't trust himself. And when you lose your confidence—he didn't know what to do from this point forward.

"I think it's stopped," Jimmy said. Nick looked over and saw big red swathes of toilet paper jammed up Jimmy's nose.

"I think so," Nick agreed.

More silence. But the boys had spoken to each other. It didn't matter what it was about—unless it was another reboot of the argument. Any unthreatening choice of words was an olive branch at this point.

"I almost had you," Jimmy said with a bloody grin.

This made Nick smile too. "You must have put on a few pounds since the last time we'd done that."

"Look," Jimmy said. He took a second to get his words, an unusual thing for the impulsive kid. "I get it. I understand why you are frustrated with me. The thing is . . . I don't know why I do it. I don't want to be a screw up. I don't like it. But it finds me. I don't think I can help it."

Nick took his brother's words seriously. It wasn't an apology. Neither one of them were likely to apologize today. But it was an acknowledgement of his actions, of reality. "Why the drugs?" Nick asked, trying not to sound like he was accusing him of anything.

"Why not?" Jimmy said quickly. Then after a pause, "Mom had those pain pills. At some point I tried them, and they made things easier. I could go on. I didn't have to feel every prick and poke the world gave me. I felt like a normal person. Almost, anyway."

"So, you're self-medicating?"

"Yeah, at first. Then I go overboard. That part I can't explain, except to say its slippery ground. When you start taking something that works—more is more. And you think, if two pills feel this good, three must feel even better."

Nick took it in. He'd suspected his younger brother of smoking pot a couple years ago when he started dressing differently. He didn't exactly have a lot of friends, but when he did hang out with people, they dressed the same druggy way: mostly dark, earthy clothes. But this was the first time—even after busting him at the grocery store—that they had openly talked about it.

"Okay," Nick said. "So, I get why you had that bottle of pills at the store, but why the candles in your other pocket?"

Jimmy smiled again. "Do you know what day it is, big brother?"

"Wednesday?" Nick said, not really sure.

"What day of the month?"

Nick's mind worked hard to access information he hadn't needed in about a week, since the update. He added the six days to the date of the update and almost got to the answer before Jimmy spelled it out for him.

"Happy birthday, Nick. You're a legal adult now."

Nick soaked in the surreal moment; he had forgotten his own birthday. But Jimmy hadn't. How could this happen? He knew their entire world had been turned upside down, but he thought he had been on top of it.

"I guess I was so focused on staying alive I totally forgot," Nick said finally. "But what were you—
"

"I didn't have a cake," Jimmy said, "so I figured a Spam cake would be in order." The two boys laughed at the ridiculous notion. What was really funny, Nick realized, was that this was reality. This was his real life. He couldn't have ever guessed he and his brother would have done what they'd done in the last week, and he certainly didn't think he'd be spending his birthday out on the Dalton Highway a hundred miles north of the arctic circle.

"Look at me," Nick said. Jimmy turned. Nick examined Jimmy's nose. "If it's broken," he said, "it's at least straight. It should heal up okay."

Jimmy nodded in approval.

"Jimmy, I don't know how to say this without sounding all gushy and Nancy-like. But when you start jonesin' for a fix—I mean, you're not actually addicted to anything are you?"

Jimmy shook his head. "I was pretty close with Mom's pills, but she ran out after she started using DataMind and I had to go cold turkey on those. That was months ago."

"And you don't really want to use them, or do you?"

"I don't like the way it turns out. But I'd be lying if I said I didn't like the way it made me feel, temporarily."

"Well, can you just let me in. Tell me what's going on, so I can help you?"

Jimmy chewed on Nick's words. "It's just that . . . I don't want to need your help. I don't want my big brother to always have to bail me out every time. There's help, and then there's something that looks like help that actually destroys a person. Like a little bird pushing itself out of the egg. If you help it, it'll never be strong enough. It'll die. You helped it to death."

Nick understood what he meant, but he regretted it being that way. What could he say? There didn't seem to be anything he could do.

"Promise me this, at least," Nick said. "Next time the King of the Hill attacks you, don't drop your gun and run. Just shoot him." Nick laughed as he said it, but he could tell Jimmy didn't find it funny. It wasn't the overly dramatic Jimmy either; it was in sincerity.

"It's not that hard, especially on that Stevens," Nick said trying to smooth out the tension. "Just cock it and pull the trigger. It's just like how Dad taught us."

"Taught you," Jimmy said.

"What are you talking about? Dad taught us both when . . ." His mind raced back for the memory. His dad used to take him outdoors: hiking, fishing, target practice at the range. But much of that dried up when Grandpa Joe died. After the divorce and by the time Jimmy and his mom came along, Nick's dad had given up the outdoor life.

"Jimmy, I just knew Dad had taught us both to shoot."

"Well, he didn't. Some of us didn't have father-son time lavished upon us." There was the old Jimmy coming back out again.

"Then let's do it now," Nick said.

"Do what now?"

"Learn to shoot."

Jimmy gave Nick an incredulous look. Nick maintained his demeanor, even got up to show Jimmy he meant it.

"We don't have that many bullets," Jimmy protested.

"It doesn't matter how many we have. If you don't know how to shoot them, they won't do you any good. And I'm counting on you to watch my back."

Jimmy did have a point, however. Nick checked his Springfield: most of two magazines and some change in his pocket. The Stevens had a dozen shells on the sling and five on the wrap around the stock.

"Let's shoot some of both," Nick decided. "First you have to know how to load it. Before you can shoot it." Nick pulled the magazine out of the nine-millimeter pistol, racked it back to unload the chambered round. Then he put the round back into the magazine, smashing his thumb hard against the resistance of the magazine's spring. He dry-fired the pistol and handed it to Jimmy.

"What do I do?"

Nick showed him how to hold the handgun, how to support his grip with his left hand. Then he showed him how to stand and aim so that his right eye lined up with the front and rear sight.

"Now, load one of these," Nick said handing him a magazine.

It was intuitive enough for Jimmy to get it in, although he first had the magazine backwards and had to adjust. He slapped it in until it clicked shut.

"Now what?"

"Now you rack it. Maintain your grip with your right hand and keep your finger off the trigger." Nick demonstrated, pointing his index finger out straight. "Then with your left hand, pull the action back."

Nick's hand gestures were only of limited help. Jimmy struggled to even figure out which part of the gun could be pulled back. Several times Nick wanted to jump in and demonstrate, but he remembered the baby bird analogy and resisted. Finally, Jimmy found the action and pulled hard. His left hand slipped off and the pistol in his right hand jerked forward.

Nick reacted in kind, twisting his feet out of the direction of the barrel. "Sorry," Jimmy pleaded.

"Don't shoot my toes, Bro," Nick said good naturedly.

Jimmy tried again, this time with more grit and determination. It was obvious to Nick that Jimmy didn't have enough strength to reliably rack it. He could do it; he was going to do it, at least once. But in a pinch, it would never be a safe bet that Jimmy could quickly load the Springfield. Nick understood this reality but didn't tell Jimmy.

With much effort, Jimmy got the action pulled all the way back. His hands were shaking with tension as he said, "What do I do with it?"

"Let go with the left hand," Nick said quickly.

The pistol slammed shut and the reflective hammer pin filled the hole below the rear sight.

"Okay, it's hot now," Nick said. "Support your grip with the left hand, and let's find a target." They looked up and down the road. "There," Nick said pointing to a speed limit sign that had already seen its share of bullet holes. "Let's see if you can hit double-nickels." That was Nick's dad's term for when the speed limit was fifty-five. Nick wondered why they even had speed limits up here. No one had any business going that fast on the Dalton, and it wasn't like anyone would ever get caught speeding and ticketed by local police anyway.

Jimmy raised the gun, aiming it with shaky hands. It seemed too heavy for him, Nick thought. "Now, take a deep breath and blow it out slowly. As you do, gently squeeze the trigger. Don't yank. Just pull gradually."

Nick plugged his ears with his fingers and waited. Despite the cool air—it had gotten noticeably cooler today—beads of sweat dripped down Jimmy's face.

The gun fired, and Jimmy nearly dropped it. Carefully, he surrendered it to Nick. With a voice elevated to overcome the ringing in his ears, Jimmy said, "I don't know, Nick. I'm not good at it."

Nick took the weapon away gingerly and looked down the road at the sign. Jimmy had missed. "That's okay," Nick said. "That's not your main firearm anyway. You're more of a shotgun kind of guy." Nick didn't look to see if Jimmy was convinced but instead went to the van and got the Stevens single-shot.

Returning, Nick said, "What you just shot is a modern, hi-tech firearm. It's taken hundreds of years to get the weapon to that point, and it only makes sense that it would be uncomfortable for a newbie shooter. This one, however…" He handed the shotgun to Jimmy. "…is beautifully simple."

Jimmy held the weapon he'd carried so many times, but it looked like he was seeing it with new eyes. Perhaps, Nick thought, he was making mental connections about the gun's mechanics after working with the pistol.

Nick had Jimmy open the breech. "Now, if there was a shell in there, it would have automatically kicked it out when you opened it. This is a good thing. It means you can reload faster."

"Just one at a time though, right?"

"That's right," Nick said. "Harder to mess that up, isn't it?"

Jimmy didn't respond but stayed focused on the weapon.

"Now, drop a shell down into the breech and close it," Nick instructed.

Jimmy did. "Is it ready to fire?" Jimmy asked.

"No, you need to pull the hammer back with your right-hand thumb."

Jimmy did easily, and the old gun clicked softly.

"It's cocked. Raise it to your shoulder, put your cheek against the stock, and aim at the sign."

Jimmy did. "There's no sights," he said in mild panic.

"That's because you don't need them on a scatter gun. Just get that forward bead over the target." Nick got behind Jimmy making sure he had the butt fully against his shoulder, firmly. "Okay, same drill. Breath out and gently squeeze."

Nick switched his focus back and forth between Jimmy and the sign, watching for errors. He looked solid.

The shotgun erupted, shoving Jimmy's shoulder. Jimmy maintained his position, the gun tight against his body.

Nick looked at the sign, punched through with a dozen new holes. Then he looked back at Jimmy who stood motionless, still aiming the gun. But there was a change: a smile spread across his brother's face.

CHAPTER 20

THE BOYS RODE hard. Nick pushed the van to its limits. The road demanded tender care, but Nick gave it little. The van bounced hard, convulsing violently as if in death throes. Nick and Jimmy had talked about it. They didn't want another flat tire, but they were close enough to Deadhorse—the last sign read ninety miles—they could probably walk the rest of the way if they had to. It would take a few days, but they could do it.

They'd already put the five gallons of gas Pete gave them in the tank. They were down to a third of a tank, but it ought to last. It had to. At this point, they just wanted to finish, to get this hellish chapter of their lives over with.

Their constant companion had been the pipeline. Sometimes it drifted away, not running perfectly parallel to the highway. Sometimes it ran behind small mountains, and when it did it seemed to

Nick like they were holding their breaths, underwater, waiting for it to reappear. It always did, usually in mere minutes.

As they traveled further north, the landscape changed. It still had picturesque fields of greenery, the kind of vistas that demanded explanation, like someone had to have planted it, cultivated it. It wasn't until you had seen these meadows swallowed up by the first snowfall that you realized how temporary they were. These grasslands were giving it their all, like a beautiful virgin who could only appear and dance one night of her life, hoping to draw in a suitor. Even in late July, there were patches of snow in the shadows behind rocks and in dips and gullies. The pockets of snow were increasing in occurrence and the terrain grew rockier and more inhospitable as they traveled.

This must have something to do with why the research station had been put up here, Nick figured, although he didn't know that for a fact. Being over two hundred miles north of the arctic circle was Deadhorse's claim to fame. This was no-man's land up here. Almost, no-creature's land.

Nick looked across the horizon, checking. In the distance, far west of the highway, he saw a couple dozen figures he believed were caribou. He'd seen on the Discovery Channel how they could dig under snow and get at lichen during the winter, the goats of the north.

For the next two hours, the boys talked little. Nick felt they didn't have to. Not since the shooting lesson. They both seemed focused on finishing. Jimmy, unusually, was onboard with the plan. To get to Deadhorse and find Bob's research station and figure it out from there. Nick, unusually, was relying on his brother. He felt like they were in it together now, more than before. Nick's worry and apprehension were still there, but those notions and emotions were quelled, pushed down below the surface. Not by a matter of will-power or choice, but because a greater more powerful idea was on top: *the end was in sight*. He didn't know what lay beyond it. He couldn't bring himself to care even if he tried. Too great, too mesmerizing was the goal, the brass ring, the finish line. He was almost there, and, against all logic and reason, he knew they would be safe at the research station

Up ahead, Nick noticed a change in the road, something hanging overhead that didn't look like the typical green interstate signs.

"This is it," Jimmy said, whose eyes proved again to be stronger than Nick's.

As they approached the rickety, must-have-been-made-in-the-fifties sign, Nick read it:

WELCOME TO DEADHORSE

Spray painted under it in smaller letters was more writing:

WELCOME TO THE END OF THE WORLD

"They didn't know how right they were," Nick said. Jimmy grinned but said nothing.

Nick reached down in the floorboard and grabbed his nine-millimeter and put it in his lap. Jimmy reflexively copied him, taking the long-barreled shotgun, and setting it up on its butt, his hand gripping the barrel. Nick wanted to warn him about dirtying the barrel with the oil on his skin and how it could make it rust, but he didn't. What did it matter anymore?

They drove under the sign and entered what could only be loosely called a town. Nick had expected—he didn't know why—some sort of pull-off from the Dalton, like an interstate exit. But this was nothing like that. The Dalton had become Main Street of this shanty town. It reminded Nick of old ghost towns out west, except instead of desert sand there was snow and asphalt everywhere. And instead of knotty-pine board-and-batten siding, the buildings were made of crude industrial materials: principally concrete block and steel.

Nick slowed down. He didn't know why. Maybe he wanted to look around, as if this was such a remote town they wouldn't have been affected by the update. The thought occurred to him that he should speed up, that there was a greater likelihood of crazies here than out on the highway, but he kept the van at fifteen miles-per-hour.

They passed one of the only intersections, a little side road that had even less reason to be called a road. Back behind one of the buildings, Nick noticed dozens of eighteen-wheelers parked side-by-side. He had witnessed the crappiest excuse for a truck-stop in the world, he told himself. He made a mental note to remember the trucks. They could be useful later, he thought. If they actually do find this station and it's not teeming with food and fuel like Bob had promised, it might be necessary to come back to the truck-stop and scavenge for supplies. Knowing his luck, the trucks would be full of deicing salt or other useless items.

Nick had an uncontrollable nose-snort laugh.

"What?" Jimmy asked.

"I'm sorry. Just had the thought: what if those trucks were full of nothing but DataMind phones?"

Jimmy grinned but raised a questioning eyebrow. "You okay, big brother?"

Nick nodded his head. It had seemed absurd to him. His mind was probably just trying to break the tension. It wasn't, however, that unlikely. DataMind had been handing out technology like candy, working their way into other industries besides their well-known apps. They were taking losses, selling mobile devices at or below cost with their mindfulness apps already pre-loaded and optimized for the operating system. At this very moment, there had to be billions of phones tainted by the DataMind app like poisoned wells. They were pieces of technology that were veritable land mines, and if they survived and rebuilt the world after this winter like the old man in the bus had said, Nick knew one of civilization's ongoing chores would be teaching the children not to play with old phones. They would have to destroy the devices one at a time for decades, and—like the World War II landmines that were still occasionally discovered on farms in Western Europe or the South Pacific—they wouldn't get them all in Nick and Jimmy's lifetimes.

A large bump jolted the boys.

"What was that?" Nick asked.

Jimmy looked in the mirror and out his window. "We're off pavement," he said.

Jimmy was right. The color of the road in front of them had turned lighter and Nick could see a dust cloud brewing behind them where the van had tossed up the more-dirt-than-gravel road. The buildings were less densely packed, and what was standing didn't look like storefronts, homes, or even like they were used regularly. Instead, they were like an ongoing industrial junkyard holding rolls of aluminum, pallets of sheet metal and lumber, and mountains of concrete blocks and rubble.

"Are we still on the Dalton?" Jimmy asked.

"I don't know. Did I miss a turn?"

Jimmy shook his head. "Bob said that we should take the Dalton until it ended. How do we know when it ends?"

"Didn't he say we couldn't miss it?" Nick asked. "This doesn't seem like…"

Just then the boys both spotted the answers they were looking for. A construction sawhorse colored orange and white waited for them fifty feet ahead. The sign read:

DO NOT ENTER
CONSTRUCTION ZONE AHEAD

Nick pulled up close, almost close enough to touch the sign with the front bumper.

"Now what?" Jimmy more said than asked.

"Now, we check to see if the coast is clear."

They did. Jimmy even climbed into the back and peered out the window. "Nothing, I can see," he reported.

Nick got out first, and Jimmy followed. Nick felt vulnerable, not so much because they were out of the car—although that always made him nervous—but because they were out of road. If they ran into trouble, they couldn't simply retreat back to the van and go on to Deadhorse. *Where would they go?*

"There's the pipeline," Nick said after walking past the construction sign. From there the road gradually shifted from dirt to grass and permafrost snow, the kind that wasn't skied on. Nick started toward the pipeline.

"Wait, what about the food?" Jimmy asked.

Nick thought for a second. "Either we find Bob and everything's good, or we'll come back to the van and figure something else out. Let's get a couple bottles of water and leave everything else." Of course, Nick didn't mean leaving their guns, and Jimmy didn't even seem to consider it. The boys stuffed water bottles, one in each pants pocket. It looked and felt silly, but they both seemed to intuit the solution as being the most practical.

Nick wandered out onto the pockets of snow that were almost ice. It cracked more than crunched under their feet. The air was warmed by the summer sun and the snow trickled in little pools and streams. But Nick knew the snow would win here, that the sun would beat down its hardest this month and part of the next but then would retreat and the snow would begin rebuilding itself, regaining all of its losses and then some.

Nick was excited to reach the pipeline again and he quickened his pace. It made no sense, but he couldn't help imagining Pete stepping out from behind one of the support piers at any moment. Where was he now? he wondered. Probably going on with his life. He had a whole village to keep going. And if anyone, any group of people could make it without the rest of the world, it was them. Nick hoped unrealistically, sentimentally that he would see Pete again. And Lusa. He had almost forgotten her, and the simple evocation of her name brought that warm, aching feeling back in his stomach.

Ten yards from the pipeline, Jimmy ran forward and slapped the giant structure making a loud ping. "Touchdown," he yelled.

A few days ago, Nick would have scolded him and tried to wound him, saying how he'd never played a day of football in his life. But today was different.

The boys traveled on dutifully, cheerfully but in complete silence. Nick knew Jimmy, undoubtedly, was contemplating the same thoughts, the brief description and instruction Bob had given them. Nick had a moment of panic that subsided as quickly as it had risen. *What if Bob didn't even live in Deadhorse and was bonkers and had made the whole thing up?* His reasoning mind came to the rescue with all the supporting evidence that was too strong to be coincidental.

The chief piece of corroborating evidence lay before them. About one hundred paces ahead, the pipeline took a sharp right-turn and headed east. Just like Bob had said, a tall mountain—Bob had called it Mount Hubley—stood ahead of them, north in the original trajectory of the pipeline. Nick didn't know why the engineers had made the pipeline veer off except, perhaps, to avoid the great bowl of a valley between them and Mount Hubley.

The boys slowed their pace. The icy snow was slick, and the valley wall was riddled with various sized rocks. Some smooth, some jagged.

When they reached the bottom, they stopped for the little stream of melted run-off. "Bob didn't mention this," Nick said pensively.

"Probably doesn't happen but a few weeks out of the year," Jimmy said.

Nick knew he was right, but his anxiety was returning. Before he got wet in this increasingly cool part of the world, he wanted to know it wasn't all for naught.

"Look there," shouted Jimmy.

Nick looked but saw nothing but the mountain. "What?"

"There it was again."

Nick realigned his focus a bit to the right where Jimmy was pointing. Then he saw it too. A distant flash of light, repeating every three seconds.

CHAPTER 21

THE BOYS WADED through the ankle-deep water. Jimmy tried to skip through it quickly as if it would somehow save him from getting wet. It didn't. And he splashed Nick in the process.

"Watch it," Nick warned.

Having crossed the stream, they were now at the bottom of the valley—water does run downhill after all. The boys headed up the gentle grade toward the blinking light. It appeared to Nick to be at the base of the mountain. So, the rest of their walk, the rest of their journey, was about to end in sight, he told himself.

They walked in silence except for the rhythmic crunching of icy snow under their feet and the deep breathing that sounded like the pace that occurred when a jogger starts running and hasn't yet fully depleted his oxygen supplies. It was harder going uphill, but Nick didn't care. This was nothing after all they had gone through.

"What do we say when we get there?" Jimmy asked as they got close enough to see features of the station, most of which consisted of a steel door that resembled a bank vault and a large bay window. The rest of the station was ostensibly inside the mountain. Either that or this was a glorified shanty shack too small for one, let alone three.

"The truth, I guess," Nick answered.

"Yeah, but it's kind of odd showing up like this, isn't it? What—do we just ring the doorbell and say, 'Hi, we're here to ride out the end of the world with you.'?"

Nick shrugged his shoulders and kept on marching. It was strange, he agreed. But this was nothing in comparison to the surrounding events of the last week. The update made this seem downright normal.

After several minutes, the boys were about fifty paces away from the station door.

"Look there," Jimmy said pointing.

Nick noticed the four white, wooden crosses sticking up out of the ground. In front of each, the snow was uncovered and black dirt was mounded up.

"Graves," Nick breathed.

"Looks like he wasn't alone after all."

The boys stood motionless letting the reality settle in. Before they were ready, the door to the station cracked open and a man with a blue coat and fur hood appeared. He raised a rifle towards them and shouted, "Identify yourselves."

Nick and Jimmy both flinched. Nick started to reach for his pistol, but his reason stopped him.

"We're Joe's grandkids," Jimmy yelled. "I'm Jimmy, and this is my brother Nick."

The man pulled back his hood as if removing a disguise. His mouth opened and his blue eyes shimmered in astonishment.

"You're Joe's boys?" he asked as he lowered his rifle. He didn't wait for them to respond but continued. "Well come on in for goodness sake." He stood sideways, his back against the open door like a concierge inviting in patron guests.

Nick and Jimmy hurried forward. They walked through the door as the man watched them. His head turned as if on a swivel, charmed by their mere existence. Nick avoided eye-contact, feeling a bit uncomfortable with the one-eighty the man had done.

As Nick followed Jimmy, he turned to watch their host enter. The man grabbed at the door and yanked hard. "This darn thing always gets hung." He grunted an old man grunt. Nick started to offer to help, but before he could the man gave another hard pull and collapsed part way to the ground, catching himself on one knee.

Nick rushed to his side. "Are you okay?"

"Yeah, just a touch of flu. I don't want to get you sick. Shouldn't be contagious as long as I've had it. Just help me to that chair, would ya?"

Nick helped him over to a kitchen table while Jimmy pulled the outside door shut. The old man sat, slouched over, and breathed hard trying to regain his strength.

Nick looked the place over: the bay windows faced the south, the way they'd come in. The table ran half the length of the room. Along one wall were kitchen appliances: a stove, microwave, fridge, freezer, sink. Beyond the table was a wall of monitors, a computer desk, and another vault-like door.

The boys stood awkwardly, waiting for the man to recover. He seemed to notice, raised an eye between hard breaths, and said, "Grab a chair, boys. You've got to be worn out." They complied. "Now don't worry about me; I've had this cold, flu—whatever the darn thing is—since the day after the update. I have these little spells, and then they pass. I've got to be close to licking this bug. Even for an old geezer like me, a week is as long as I ever get sick."

Despite the fact Bob was sitting down, Nick could tell he was a tall, large framed man. He looked like he could have played football fifty years ago. He had thinning gray-brown hair pulled back, and he wore large out-of-style glasses.

"The name's Bob Cox," he continued. "You can call me Bob. That, or Supreme Chancellor and Viceroy to the Galactic High Command. Your choice." He erupted into laughter that turned into more coughing, then a final wheeze. "Sorry, I've gone a little stir-crazy up here by myself."

Nick noticed one of Bob's eyes didn't look right. He couldn't tell if it was a glass eye or if he'd had an injury. Maybe it was a lazy eye that was never corrected, he thought.

"That's okay," Jimmy responded. "I think we've all been pushed hard this last week."

"Right you are," Bob said. He looked at the two of them for a minute. Again, the awkward feeling returned to Nick. "Say, you boys have wet feet. Take those boots off and dry out."

Nick had reservations about doing so. He hoped Bob was just a loony grandfather-type character, but he felt misgivings about setting up camp just yet. But the need to dry his feet was real and his inner doubts could be imaginary, he told himself.

The two yanked off their dripping wet shoes, and Jimmy tugged off his socks. Nick, having had larger concerns, had nearly forgotten he had been sockless this whole-time. Nick was keenly aware of how bad he smelled, and he was sure Jimmy was no better. The station smelled like a box of roses, probably not from any kind of perfume or air freshener

239

but just from an actually clean and well-kept environ. They'd slid gradually from the world of sanitized society into the dirty, brutish existence of no running water and no electricity over the course of a week. But they had returned into the artificial, civilized, clean world in a single moment. It was shocking and made Nick feel more than unclean. He felt like a leper that ought to be calling out, warning those around him.

Bob, apparently feeling better, got up. After putting his rifle on a wall rack, he disappeared through the door in the back of the room.

Nick looked at Jimmy questioningly, trying to get a read on the old man through his brother's eyes.

"What?" Jimmy whispered.

Nick tilted his head in the direction Bob had gone. "Does he seem . . . normal?"

"As normal as anybody who lost four people in the update and who had to live alone this whole time," Jimmy answered too loudly.

Bob returned with a stack of towels in his arms. "You guys think I'm kooky, don't ya? Well, don't worry. I'll put this one to rest," he said as he divided the towels between the two of them. "I *am* crazy. But I didn't go broke during the update, if that's what's got you worried. I've been crazy since at least the last century." He laughed again at his own commentary.

"We didn't mean any disrespect," Jimmy volunteered. "We've just been leery of people this week. Especially my brother." They both looked at Nick with suspicion. "But it's his cautiousness that has kept us alive."

That's right, Nick thought but didn't say. More than that, even. It was Jimmy's half-cocked approach to life that had nearly gotten them killed.

"I take it by what I over-heard that you two noticed the graves outside."

They nodded.

"Co-workers. No, friends. Even the ones I didn't like. They were my friends." Tears welled up in his eyes. Then a glimmer. "Hey, that reminds me, strangely enough. You boys want steaks for dinner?"

Bob hobbled quickly to the fridge and took out a big plastic pan with marinating steaks. Nick had the horrid notion that he was staring at the tenderloins of Bob's deceased friends, Hannibal Lector-style.

Bob seemed to sense his trepidation. "It's caribou. It's what I was doing when the update happened. Hunting. You know, a few drift up here despite the snow. They're stupid that way. They ought to stay further south where the grasses grow more plentifully. But they like digging up lichen, I think. Anyway, I'd taken a small calf and was dragging out the choice cuts when I saw Fred running towards me from the station. At first, I thought he was coming to warn me. That there was something wrong, that there was an emergency. Well, there was something wrong, but he wasn't coming to tell me. Thank God I had that hunting rifle with me." He pointed to the rear wall where he had returned the rifle onto a wall rack.

"So, what do ya say?" Bob asked presenting the steaks closer. "I'll fry potatoes, and…" He set the tray of steaks down on the counter and rushed back to the fridge. "Yes. I still got it. Cherry pie for dessert."

"Sounds good," Nick said. It didn't matter they'd had caribou at Pete's village. These steaks looked like different critters entirely. That was the thing about civilization: the food. The food was so good. The same food prepared in all these different, wonderful ways. He felt himself relax a bit, easing into this obviously more comfortable habitation.

"Say, Bob?" Jimmy asked.

Bob looked up with a playful expression. He seemed to like someone calling his name.

"Is there a shower we could use? My brother really stinks."

"Hey, so do you," Nick added.

"We've got the hottest showers in Alaska," Bob assured them. "When the government built this place, they dug down into the earth and installed geo-thermal heating. Run them all you like, you'll never run out of hot water."

Bob took the boys through the vault-door. It led to a long hallway that branched off into multiple halls and doors. Nick thought he could get lost down

242

there. They reached a bathroom that was more like a locker room at the gym.

"Wait here just a sec," Bob said as he hobbled out the door. He returned before Nick or Jimmy could start a conversation. "Here you go," he said handing them a bunch of blue sweatpants and sweatshirts. "These are as close to uniforms as we wear here. There's some clean—I promise they're washed—underwear and t-shirts in there too. Had to guess on your sizes. You two look to be similar in size to Jamison."

The boys thanked him, and Bob said he would be cooking and to return out front when they got done.

The hot shower beat against their skin like a pressure-washer getting off sidewalk stains. Nick didn't remember rolling in the dirt, but the brown puddles at his feet would suggest otherwise. Then there was the soap. Oh, glorious invention of mankind! How had anyone been happy before soap? he thought.

The showers were open stalls with no curtains. Nick was used to this set-up from football, so it didn't bother him. To his surprise, Jimmy didn't seem to care either. Maybe it was just the very physiological response from the warm water that had taken him out of his self-consciousness. Or maybe it was exhaustion. Nick didn't know. It didn't matter. They'd made it. Jimmy could be safe here. They both could.

After luxuriously long showers—they probably didn't last fifteen minutes—the boys dried off and headed back toward the kitchen. That was the word for the room that Bob had used, although to Nick the room seemed like it served far more purposes than just cooking and eating.

The spread on the table exceeded Nick's expectations. Condiments! Like soap, he wondered how people had lived without them. Bob seemed to have every kind of seasoning, sauce, and spice imaginable. And there was salad. For the first time in both their lives, the boys dug into a big salad and enjoyed every bite. No doubt, their bodies were craving micronutrients and roughage.

Part way through the first bites of steak, Bob jumped up from the table. "I forgot," he said.

More hobbling to the fridge and freezer. "You kids like root beer?" Ordinarily, Nick didn't like being called a kid. Today it felt good. They shook their heads yes, enthusiastically.

Bob pulled out frosted mugs from the freezer and poured fuzzy brew into them. He proudly slapped them down on the wooden table, letting it make the cracking sound like a baseball bat hitting a line-drive.

He handed off the mugs but didn't take his seat. Instead, he looked out the window as if he was watching for something in particular.

"It's been a cold summer. You two know that, don't ya?" He didn't wait for a reply. "I don't suspect it will be so cold next year. If all the reactors across the U.S. melt down, it's going to throw off some major heat, not to mention radiation."

He turned to face the table. "Hey, did you know which year we saw the most polar ice melt?" Again, no waiting. "The same year Fukushima went critical. Who knows, boys, if they all go you may be standing in the Havana of the North."

Bob had a goofy grin as he sat down to his supper. It must have been infectious, because Jimmy soon beamed. Nick figured he liked the notion of their new home becoming a tropical paradise. But Nick wasn't so sure.

"What about radiation?" Nick asked.

"Eh, I don't know," Bob said casually. "From everything I've read, it moves with the currents which tend to go from west to east at the same or similar latitude. The famous exception would be the Gulf Stream that carries warm air up to the UK. That's why they are further north than Germany but experience milder temps. They're screwed, by the way."

"But not us?"

Another shrug from Bob. "Probably not. I mean there's that one reactor in eastern Russia: Bilibino, I think it's called. It's over a thousand miles west of here, and from the few shortwave contacts I've made over there, it seems like they're keeping their lights on better than we are. You know the Russians; they're distrustful of anything that makes them happy. And that includes something like DataMind."

"Looks like they were right. I mean—about this," Nick said.

They all nodded, agreeing.

The meal was delicious, and the boys made sure Bob heard their praises. After dinner, Bob rose and went to the front door. He worked the handle. "Got to lock out the world while we sleep," he said.

After the dishes were all placed in the sink, Bob asked, "Ready to turn in?"

Nick was tired but didn't really feel sleepy. He looked for a time, for a clock somewhere. The timer on the microwave blinked asking to be reset.

"I guess," Jimmy answered.

"Alright, I'll show you to your quarters. You two don't mind having separate bedrooms, do ya?"

A new flood of good emotions arose in Nick. "Are you kidding? I'm tired of looking at that jerk." He looked straight at Jimmy so he could tell he was kidding.

"At least I don't fart in my sleep," Jimmy answered.

More laughter from Bob. Apparently, he wasn't too old for fart jokes. Nick could imagine him letting some big, juicy wet ones, too. Nasty old-man farts. Nick made himself laugh.

Bob escorted them past the vault-door, turned and locked it behind him, like he had the entrance door. "Can't take any chances," he said. "I'd be really surprised if any crazies drifted this far north, but if they do and they break through the glass to get in, they'll have six inches of solid steel to contend with." The word *steel* seemed to stick in his mouth. He stopped what he was doing and darted back into the kitchen, seconds later returning with his rifle. "I sleep just a little better with this by my side."

The boys nodded, understanding. They had their weapons too. This place was a veritable fortress, but it would be a long time before Nick could imagine being comfortable without his Springfield.

Nick closed the door to his room and dove into his bed. It was little more than a cot with olive drab wool blankets and thin cotton sheets underneath. Beside the bed was a small table with a reading lamp. He clicked on the lamp and jumped up to turn off the overhead light. When he did his left ankle shot up a twang of pain. At first he grimaced, but then that memory of trying to jump the creek came back to him and he smiled.

He clicked off the lights and returned to bed. He knew he was tired, but he didn't realize how much so or how quickly he would start the drift toward

Neverland. It was like his night at Pete's village, except he didn't need whisky to make his head feel like it was floating away from his body.

He thought of Lusa. She was gone now, a million miles away. And so was the warm feeling he had felt when he pictured her. She was just some girl in some dirty village with no hot water, no showers, no condiments, and no pie.

His last conscious thought was that she had made it. He and Jimmy had actually made it. And Bob was who he said he was, and the station was even better than promised. Hope and optimism filled his soul. Victory.

CHAPTER 22

BREAKFAST WAS ANOTHER wonderful meal: eggs sunny-side-up, bacon, toast, orange juice. All hot or cold. All on purpose.

"Well, boys," Bob said, "you better enjoy this stuff while it lasts."

"I thought you said you had years of food here," Nick said.

"Yeah, food. But not this food. The stuff they give us for the winters is a lot less sexy than this fare. We've probably got eggs until December—they last a really long time under refrigeration. Then it will be frozen egg beaters. Bacon will last until spring. So will the frozen OJ and bread. But the fresh stuff like that salad you all had last night—that's going away pretty soon. And unless the lights come back on everywhere after this winter in a really dramatic way, that might be the last salad you see. Maybe ever.

Who's to say the next iteration of society is going to go bonkers over vegetables, raw ones at that?"

"But you've got plenty of frozen food?" Jimmy asked.

"Are you kidding? At the beginning of summer, those trucks start arriving. You probably parked at the edge of town just like they do. From there, they use ATVs to drag in supplies that are meant to last us two-full years without getting restocked. And that's for a full crew of five. I'd say between us—especially if we bag more caribou—we could easily stretch it three or four years before we have to figure something else out."

"And maybe the government will resupply us next summer," Jimmy said.

"Don't hold your breath." Bob gestured toward the wall where his radio equipment was. "From everything I'm hearing, there is no United States government at the moment. There may be a faction of individuals who decide they want to resurrect one—and that's if the continental US isn't glowing from radiation, which I can't tell yet if it will be—but who's to say they'll know, remember, or even care about some little research station located at the end of the world. They'll have their hands full without us to worry about."

"And lights? We've got power for how long?" Nick asked.

"For longer than we have food; that's for sure. I don't get these military types. They send us more diesel for our generators—they even send backup generators—than they send food. It's like they want this station to go on living more than they do the workers."

All immediate questions answered, the boys hurried to help load the dishwasher. Nick felt it was the least they could do. He knew they would soon find their place here. It was ironic how back at home, they had begrudged every chore handed down to them. But here, with a relative stranger, they were clamoring for responsibilities, for something that let them earn their keep and prove their worth.

After loading up the dishwasher, Nick turned and noticed Bob was not well. He sat in his chair slumped over and sweating profusely.

"Bob, what's the matter?" Jimmy said as he rushed to his side.

"Ah, it's that darn bug again. I woke up this morning feeling like it was behind me. But here I go again."

To Nick's eye, Bob looked worse than yesterday, not better. His mind raced for a diagnosis and solution to this problem. Didn't old people die from pneumonia all the time? How could you tell when it's that instead of the flu? He didn't know, but he sure as heck didn't want their only friend in the world to die on them.

Bob went into a coughing frenzy. It didn't sound like there was phlegm in his chest. Instead, it was a dry, barking cough. He seemed to writhe in pain as the spasmodic coughs ebbed to higher and higher extremes.

After there was a lull in the storm, Bob looked up with weary eyes. "Could you help me back to bed?" he pleaded.

"I got you," Jimmy said.

Nick watched as his brother half-carried Bob through the vault-door. On the wall-screen to the left, Nick saw Bob and Jimmy's images on the monitors. He watched as they made their way to Bob's quarters.

Jimmy turned to the camera and gave a thumbs-up. Nick caught himself starting to return the gesture and felt stupid for doing so.

Nick saw Jimmy go to his bedroom, which wasn't in the same wing as Bob's. Apparently, he wanted peace and quiet even if it meant being surveilled. That was fine with Nick. They could all use some alone time.

Nick thought back to Grandpa Joe's basement. This station wasn't entirely unlike it with its even more powerful shortwave radio and the distinct earthen smell, especially deeper into the station. This place was like Grandpa's basement on steroids. Everything Nick and Jimmy had pretended it was when they were little and everything they wished it had been a week ago.

Nick thought about going to his room or maybe taking another hot shower. He couldn't though. He felt like somebody needed to stand guard. Someone had to be at the wheel, at least during the day. It was okay, he figured, to shut the whole station down and lock both doors from the inside at night. But during the day . . .

Nick stood up and walked to the bay window and looked out. The sun shined brightly, bouncing its rays off the slick, reflective melting snow and into the station. Nick wished he had sunglasses. It was a reminder of how inhospitable the outside world really was. Like it was threatening him, even now. Warning him that it had more where that came from and that he and his brother better learn their lesson and stay indoors.

Anthropomorphizing nature seemed silly, but the sense was palpable and real. Nick talked back silently, telling the old hag that he had no beef with her. That he was just trying to stay alive and that she needed to move on and pick on somebody else.

Nick touched his Springfield, tucked into his waistband behind him. It felt good. Like a dependable friend that didn't talk back and never gave him trouble. It had been a companion, a more reliable one than his own brother.

Sensing and being repulsed by the level of neuroticism he was engaging in, Nick broke away from the window post and wandered back to the desk. He'd seen the monitors on the wall, had admired them, but he'd only given a passing interest in all the other gear. Might as well get acquainted, he told himself. He'd be spending a long time here and the scenery outside wasn't exactly awe-inspiring. The radio unit, he decided, would be his outlet, his entry into the outer world that didn't require risking life or limb.

The gear was more modern than Grandpa Joe's old Zenith Trans-Oceanic 3000. But he figured it out, or so he told himself. He flipped a couple of switches that didn't seem to do anything. Instinctively, he switched them back, not wanting to change anything he didn't understand.

Another switch flipped, there was a sudden hiss coming from the headset lying on the desk. He picked it up and put it on. Now, to change the station, he thought. He knew that HAMs didn't use that vocabulary, but old habits die hard. On the computer screen in front of him, there was a virtual radio kit on screen. It looked more like Grandpa Joe's analog unit. Nick smiled. Bob was an old sentimental sap, using new stuff but trying to reference the old ways.

Nick clicked on a couple tabs that stuck out from the virtual dial. The knobs on the screen moved quickly and Nick heard the static subside. Then talking. Another language. Chinese, he thought.

He clicked another tab and found Russian.

On the third try, he heard a language that was his own. His own, if you count Canadian English and Southern US English as the same language.

You should have seen that old boy when I popped him. He barely flinched at first, but when his legs wouldn't move—I probably shot through his spine, you know—whooey, did he freak.

{You're going to get yourself killed like that.}

Oh, don't be dramatic. I was just putting it out of its own misery.

{Sounds like you were trying out your toy guns to me.}

You're just jealous. You'd be doing the same if your country hadn't outlawed everything but a pea-shooter decades ago.

A loud bang startled Nick. He yanked off his headset and turned looking for an intruder.

The sound had come from nearby, he knew. It was the deep, low frequencies that you feel vibrate through the floor and up your legs as much as you hear them.

The entrance to the station was unchanged and he couldn't see anyone or anything out the window.

Knowing he hadn't imagined the sound, he searched the room.

Right in front of him was the answer: the vault door leading to the quarters was closed shut.

CHAPTER 23

NICK RAN TO the door and pulled. It was locked and didn't budge. Had he missed someone? Did someone sneak into the station while he had his back turned listening to shortwave?

He looked at the wall of screens, trying to spot an intruder. It took only moments to scan the thirty or so screens before he saw a figure. Motionless at first, then moving slowly.

It was Bob. He was still near the vault-door. He must have closed it, Nick figured.

Nick ran to the door and yelled, "What are you doing? Bob, open the door." Nick tugged again, making sure he had twisted the handle hard enough to prove it was really locked.

Bob didn't answer. Nick looked again at the screens. Bob moved strangely, unsteadily on his feet. Nick first thought it was delirium, that the fever was making him not think straight. That would have passed the logic test if it wasn't for one thing: Bob was carrying his hunting rifle.

Nick reeled from the visual. This didn't make sense. He searched the screens for clues. He found the monitor that had Bob's quarters on it. There was his bed, his stuff. Nick almost moved on, but his eye caught something on-screen.

He grabbed the computer mouse hoping he was making the right assumption about how it worked. He moved the cursor onto the security feed and selected the one from Bob's room. Then it appeared larger on the screen. He clicked the zoom function and pulled up the white object on Bob's bed.

An overwhelming sense of helplessness flooded Nick's body and mind. There before him was a phone but not just any phone. It was one of the sold-at-cost DataMind models.

Additionally, there were earbuds connected. Bob had used the app. Bob used the update.

Nick didn't have time to think, and his usually rational mind felt frozen, stuck.

Jimmy! Where was he?

Nick found the feed of his brother's room. Jimmy lay on the bed, his feet up and his eyes closed. He had his earbuds in listening, no doubt, to his dad's music.

Nick wanted to scream, to warn him but he knew there was no way for him to hear his cry. Not through that door or through that maze-like hallway or his earbuds.

Nick watched Bob. He was obviously not thinking right. No one that went broke did. But Nick didn't understand why he was functioning as well as he was, why he was moving down the hallway checking rooms methodically. Nick thought that all the crazies were simply that: nut-jobs that had no mission or person. Just pure hatred and rage.

But that wasn't totally accurate. The King of the Hill had retained some unique qualities. And Bob had just now used the update. Who knew how long it took before the full effects took hold. That might explain why he was carrying the gun and acting purposefully.

Two of the monitors went gray with static. Nick watched as Bob moved into the frame. He was disconnecting the feed, Nick realized as he saw Bob reach another section of conduit, kneel down, and yank at wires.

Four more feeds went blank.

He had to warn Jimmy. But the camera only worked one way. He could watch, but he couldn't transmit images. Then the thought occurred: a station this big and well-designed has to have some kind of PA system.

Nick grabbed a microphone attached to a transceiver that looked like a CB radio that truckers used.

"Jimmy. Jimmy, if you can hear this. Bob used the update. He's got his gun and is…"

Nick heard voices coming through the headphones sitting on the desk. He put them on.

"Who is this? What's your handle?" the voice asked.

Stupid idiot! Nick thought. He had picked up the shortwave transceiver microphone by mistake. He looked at the monitors. Bob had pulled another junction box. More monitors were out.

Then he saw Bob change his MO. Something caught his eye around the corner. Nick could barely see past the doorway, but he saw enough to guess what Bob was after. It was the generator.

Nick frantically looked for another microphone. To his left, he found one that looked different. It had its own base and stood upright on the desk. He grabbed it, squeezed the button on its handle, and spoke into its microphone.

"Jimmy, Bob is coming. He's gone broke, and he has a gun." He looked up at Jimmy's monitor.

Jimmy had heard something. He pulled out one of his earbuds as if to investigate.

Nick repeated himself. "Jimmy, Bob's coming with a gun. He's going to try to kill you."

A brief second showed Jimmy sitting upright. But then Nick heard a shot and the whole array of monitors, lights, all the electricity went down.

"That's it," Nick said aloud. "He killed the generator."

He stared helplessly at the black screen where he'd last seen his brother. Jimmy had heard him. Nick was sure of it. But did Jimmy understand?

Nick moved through the kitchen like a bandit ransacking the place, overturning everything in sight looking—not for valuables to steal—but for some tool, some key, anything to get the door open.

He pulled his Springfield out. Maybe he could shoot a hole through the door, he thought. But even his maxed-out, freaked-out, emotion-riddled mind knew better than to think he could shoot through six inches of steel. More likely the bullet would ricochet back and kill him.

Slowly, in desperate little lunges that felt like his feet were made of lead, he moved to the vault-door. He laid his head against it, feeling its cold. But he was white-hot with exasperation. Tears joined his sweat and traced down his cheeks onto the cold, hard steel door.

A shot rang out.

CHAPTER 24

ALONE, SITTING ON a bar stool, Nick sipped his coffee and looked out the bay window. Nick never thought of himself as a coffee drinker, but when winter came this year, the hot brew seemed inviting enough to try. In a week's time, he'd become a pot-a-day drinker.

Behind him came the chatter that had become his constant companion. The sound of the living. The sound of the holdouts who had made it through the first summer and fall after the update. He didn't transmit, not because he didn't have a proper handle—who cared about that anymore besides the dyed in the wool HAMs anyway—but because he didn't want to talk with the outside world. He was content to merely listen and observe. The world he was in was not the one of his youth. There was no guarantee that anyone would be hospitable. Common decency was an oxymoron, right up there with common sense.

He refilled his cup. It was his second of the day, and he thought it was his favorite. Each cup had a different feeling, a different character, he believed. The first slapped you awake. The second got your synapses firing and all the optimism going. The third and fourth were just echoes of the second, attempts to keep the party going a little longer.

He crooked his head so he could see out the window and to the left. The recent snow fall had covered the grave sites, making the newest grave indistinguishable from the four that had preceded it. Even the little white cross serving as a headstone was identical to the others. Nick had trouble remembering which was the new one. *I should have put his name on it,* he thought.

He drank deeply from his cup, the black liquid threatening to burn his tongue. He swished it away into his cheeks attempting to minimize the damage, then swallowed it when it became bearable. Now he was feeling it. The buzz, the sparkling sensation that came when his brain began to dance.

What he'd do without his new-found addiction, he didn't know. That's what had happened to Bob, he figured. He was just as addicted to the DataMind app as all the other researchers were but had missed the update while he was gone hunting. He must have come back, realized what had gone wrong, and tried his hardest to give up the app cold-turkey. A week out and he was as miserable as ever.

Everyone has a breaking point, a moment when right and wrong don't seem to matter. Bob went broke before he used the update. The app had broken him long before; he just hadn't known it.

The winters in Alaska were always long, cold, and hard to bear. But this one would be the hardest. He had to endure until spring when all of man's hopes and anticipations would be tested. Would Bob's predictions come true? Would they be living in the Havana of the North soon? Only time would tell. One thing Nick knew was that he had an important role to play, one more important than just surviving.

In the weeks following the incident with Bob, Nick had made a formal survey of the station. He had started with getting the spare generator up and running. Then he had worked on the food supply, measuring and calculating the caloric contents to see exactly how long he could last there.

By shear accident, he had discovered the repository. There was a reason the doors were shaped like bank vaults; the whole station was a complex for storing and preserving ancient or heirloom seeds. Grains, vegetable seeds, even seeds for fruit and nut trees had all been catalogued and preserved in the St. Victoria Research Station.

If the records were accurate, there were over forty tons and over three-thousand varieties of seeds saved in the mountain. Forced to, Nick could live out his days on the many lifetimes of calories represented by this cache.

The questions on Nick's mind were, what would come next and how should this asset that was invisible to the rest of the world be tapped and utilized? It was far more valuable as starter seed than as direct food. Judiciously distributed, it could reboot the entire planet's agricultural system, one farm at a time.

He looked back out the window, this time toward the horizon. On good days, he could see the pipeline in the distance. But today the snow blurred his view.

Nick saw a figure emerge somewhere close to the valley's now frozen river. It was as if this person stepped through white curtains and onto center stage. The man slumped over, carrying a rifle in one hand and dragging part of an animal carcass with the other.

Jimmy dropped the carcass and gazed toward the station knowing Nick was watching. He pulled up his snow visor and smiled. Nick reflexively grinned, recognizing the signal: his brother had been successful and needed help dragging home the kill.

Nick rushed to put his shoes and coat on. In his haste, he slammed his cup down hard, spilling big black drops. He stopped, hesitated, looking deeply into the black liquid. It had been the blackness, the dark that he and Jimmy had looked into. Not because they chose to or wanted to, but because they had been held down against their will and forced to.

He wondered how he was still alive and, of all places, alive here. He wondered how his brother had become a man and the one person Nick knew he could truly trust.

This was the end of something. The old world. The old way of life. The update had come like a plague wiping out untold millions. What it left—who it left— was what mattered now. Not who was gone.

This was the end of the world, and Nick wondered why he felt so alive.

THE END

The story continues in *Last Refuge:* book 2 in *The Final Update Series.*

If you haven't done so, please sign up for my newsletter: https://www.subscribepage.com/b7x8r2 In addition to receiving announcements about new releases, deals, and writing updates, you'll also get a free short story!

Also, if you enjoyed this book, please consider leaving an honest review. It's about the nicest thing you can do for an author. And I'd like to thank you personally if you decide to leave one. Shoot me an email and let me know how awesome you are: info@allenkuzara.com

Author's Note

September 7th, 2018

Run from Ruin was my fourth novel or, depending on how you look at it, my first. When I finished the *Anti Life* trilogy, I felt a huge wave of relief. I had done it, something I feared I couldn't do, and I was happy with it, at least the story itself. My craft or lack thereof was another thing entirely. But I knew the bones of the story were good, and I'd gotten them down on the page.

But soon, new fears rushed in, namely that I wouldn't be able to write another novel. That might seem silly, but I wondered if the *Anti Life Series* was just the only story I had inside me, something akin to the Great American Novel, a myth that suggests just that.

Well, I had a notion for another story. I've noticed as I get older, the way forward often seems to be going backward. I remember reading a similar thought by Ray Bradbury in his excellent collection of essays: *Zen in the Art of Writing*. My childhood and adolescent memories, dreams, and fantasies all seem charged with power when I revisit them: like unplanted seeds, charged points of potential, places where my life could have changed but didn't. In the end, we're defined by these kinds of moments. The dreams we let wither and die seem just as important as the ones we chase after. Is it possible to follow *all* of your dreams? Should you? Can you be a theoretical physicist, comedian, Alaskan hermit, world-class musician, the next Michael Jordan, *and* write science fiction? Sometimes you have to trade in the good for the best. But sometimes we make the wrong trade, and sometimes we just give up.

One fantasy that had been buried deep (and it's good I never tried to execute) came from late middle school. I remember the old classroom TVs mounted up near the ceiling that always looked like they could fall off at any moment and kill someone. For some reason (maybe it was so they wouldn't have to teach us) middle school teachers allowed us to watch a program called *Channel 1* each morning. It was a news segment with young-looking anchors and hosts telling us all about world events.

BORING!!!

Don't get me wrong. It was preferable over listening to teachers ramble on about something they'd already taught us two grades before. But it still felt like brainwashing, gas lighting, forced indoctrination, or whatever you want to call it.

It was during one of these broadcasts that I first heard about nuclear disasters. What would I do if that were to happen near me? I wondered. Like all unhappy little children, I fantasized about running away. But instead of loading up a bag of luggage with cookies, my favorite stuffed animals, and extra pairs of socks, I made more sophisticated albeit equally ridiculous plans.

The fantasy must have gone on for weeks, because I also remember being influenced by shows I watched at my grandmother's house. See, she had cable, and I grew up in the boonies where we were lucky to pick up three network channels, and that was if one of us went outside and twisted the antenna pole. So, as often as I could, I went to her house to spend the night. Not only would I stay up all night watching TV, she'd feed me anything I wanted, which usually consisted of pizza, soda, and Crunch-N-Munch. How did I survive adolescence with any teeth remaining?

It was at Grandma's I remember watching an episode on the Discovery Channel, I think, about cars outfitted with bulletproof glass and special flaps for sticking a gun barrel out the vehicle and firing back at assailants.

So here goes my fantasy: A nuclear attack is imminent. My best bud Shawn and I would take off together. Who needs family, right? Hey, it's my fantasy, and I didn't know I'd have to answer to readers decades later. So…Shawn and I would take a van— much like the one parked in my Grandmother's garage (yes, it was her house and her dingy basement that I imagined Nick and Jimmy living in at the beginning of *RfR*.) We would load the van with guns and supplies as well as two Kawasaki Ninja motorcycles.

Now, I know nothing about motorcycles, and except for the dirt bike I couldn't get out of first gear in eighth grade, I've never even ridden one. But all I needed to know about Ninja motorcycles I had learned from TV commercials, namely that they had a top speed of over 200 miles-per-hour.

Back to the plan: we would travel north by van toward Canada. Who knew, maybe we'd even make it to Greenland, which looked close by on the map. Then, if we got stuck in gridlock traffic or we realized the bombs were dropping on our heads we'd jump on the bikes and make a mad dash. In my stupid thirteen year old mind, we could simply travel at 200-plus miles per hour and would reach Canada in mere hours. Simple as that.

So, obviously Nick and Jimmy didn't go to Canada, and they already lived pretty far north. But this is where the whole story came from. Instead of a friend, Nick brought his brother Jimmy who ends up being both his antagonist and ally. In truth, both boys are parts of myself. I have Nick's critical attitude, but I also have Jimmy's naïve, romantic spirit. And the two war within me all the time.

So, fearing the *Anti Life Series* was all I had in me and that I was a one-trick pony, I plotted out *Run from Ruin* as quickly as possible. I told myself it would be a novella, which gave me courage to write it. And I wrote it as fast as I could then, believing I could fix everything in the editing phase. Obviously, it turned into a short novel and not just a stand-alone but the first in the *Final Update* series. It also was a cleaner first draft than any of the *Anti Life* books had been and was written in a shorter time. I had been struggling to hit 1,000 words per day before, but during *Run from Ruin* I saw my averages climb to around 1,500. So often we are limited by self-imposed limits, and *RfR* helped me break through some of mine.

Thanks sincerely for reading this story and my scribblings about it. I had a blast writing them.

Until next time,

AK

Printed in Great Britain
by Amazon

'02R00161